# STRANDED WITH THREE BOYS

## ROYAL HAREM
## BOOK THREE

# LEXIE MIERS

# CHAPTER 1

## ERIN

It was the last day of all last days.

Even as I announced that to myself, I realized it sounded a lot more morose than it was. But there was no denying the fact that my heart firmly believed that without the safety of our Ibiza vacation, things were going to fall apart for us. For Henryk, Silas, Viktor and me. And the truth was, it made me want to stay on vacation forever.

But we had obligations. Jobs. Things we needed to get back to. Henryk had no choice in his For-God-and-Country lifestyle, either.

Real life was a bitch.

Ibiza had given us time away. A place to be ourselves. To indulge in our desires and needs. Every damned thing we wanted. Once we all arrived back in Lichtenstein, we wouldn't have the same sort of freedom.

This was officially the last of our days together, so I couldn't believe they were all still sleeping. We hadn't spent our last night wrapped around one another. We'd squandered our last opportunity to be together.

I walked onto the terrace with my cup of hotel coffee and stared out at the sun rising over the horizon. The sky was painted in shades of orange and gold as the night faded away. On any other day, I would have appreciated the beauty, but today it was bittersweet. This would be the last sunset I would see from my terrace in Ibiza. The thought tainted the colors and beauty displayed in front of me.

By tomorrow lunchtime, we'd be back in Lichtenstein, where Henryk would once again put his royal duties first. And for us three mortals, our responsibilities would soon be nagging at us to return home. Silas and Viktor ran a company that had been without them for two weeks. Henryk was about to become king. And regardless of my decision to leave or stay in Lichtenstein with Henryk, I had choices to make as well.

Henryk was the only one who didn't have to make one. His whole life had been planned out for him before he was even born.

One of the bedroom doors opened, and Silas walked out, his boxers slung low on his hips, his short hair mussed and his eyes heavy with sleep. Instead of going straight for the coffee, he walked onto the terrace and slid his arms around my waist. He pulled me into him and pressed a kiss against the side of my throat. My head tilted automatically, as if I'd been conditioned by desire to do so

"Good morning," he murmured, his breath tickling my skin.

I would have turned into him, but my eyes were pooled with tears, and I didn't want him to see them. "Morning." My voice was little more than a whisper because it was all I could manage.

He gave me a quick squeeze, the strength of his huge body feeling comforting against mine.

I wanted him. No, I needed him this morning. I turned to face him and let my hands rest on the bare skin over his heart. The quiet thumping beneath my palm quickened as I curled my fingers in the hair on his chest. He lowered his head and kissed me, stroking the small of my back through my sundress. The halter top tied around the back of my neck, and he tugged it free with one hand.

The top of the dress fell to my waist, and I was suddenly naked from the waist up. Silas bent me backward over his arm, then he lowered his head to take one of my nipples into his mouth. Pleasure skittered through me as he swirled his tongue around the tight nub of my nipple then pulled it into his mouth.

I moaned softly as he sucked hard for a moment, nipped my flesh lightly with his teeth, then again soothed the little ache with his tongue.

Oh, God, this was too good.

He laid me across the table on the terrace where we'd eaten the night before and then lifted my dress. I gasped at the coldness against my flesh but opened my legs for him.

Silas slid his hand into my panties and moved his finger over my clit. I gasped again as a jolt of pleasure lit up my belly. He moaned against my skin, and the sound went straight to my pussy.

I lifted my head and looked up and there stood Viktor beside me, his massive cock in his hand. He was almost close enough I could flick it with my tongue. He watched Silas move down my body until he was on his knees, and my legs were over his shoulders.

From the first second Silas' tongue grazed over my clit, I was thrown into a world of pleasure. I looked up at Viktor through slitted eyes. He was still watching Silas and me while stroking his cock. "Please," I begged and opened my mouth. I just wanted a taste. A distraction so I wouldn't come too soon.

Silas' fingers slid up inside me, and I cried out. His tongue teased and probed and tantalized my clit. Viktor stepped closer, and I finally got the taste I so desperately craved. His cock was long and hard in my mouth and almost more than I could take. I moaned from somewhere deep in my soul and Viktor curled his fingers into my hair, giving a tug, and the sensation went straight to my pussy.

I wanted to tell him to do it again, but I couldn't. Thankfully, I didn't need to. He gave another tug, and I smiled around his dick, murmuring another moan. I liked watching him watch me. His face changed, eyes closed, head fell back. Then a second later, he was intently staring again as I took him deeper into my throat.

I sensed Henryk watching before I saw him, before my eyes landed on him as he watched without joining in. He held my gaze, making no move to come closer, so I amped up my moans, grinding my hips against Silas' hand, against his mouth, locking my legs around his head as the pleasure spiraled through me, and Viktor's cum shot into my throat in spurts of heat and desire.

Silas, who'd been stroking his cock with his free hand, moved to stand on the other side of me, and I turned my head to take him into my mouth as he came hard and fast, his body spasming, his breath shuddering.

When he finished, I sat up, and Henryk's scowl deepened the lines on his face. "You broke your coffee mug." He turned and walked back into the suite. I looked at Silas then at Viktor, but none of us moved to follow. I was still half-naked on the table, so I pulled my halter top up and pushed my skirt down. Then I slid off the table and walked inside on shaky legs to find Henryk.

He'd obviously moved all the way through and out the front door. Certainly, he wasn't mad that he'd woken to find me having an orgasm with Silas and Viktor. After everything we'd done together and separately from them, Henryk knew how this worked.

I slipped on a pair of sandals and headed out to find him. He wasn't in the coffee shop or the common area lobby, the gym, the pool area, the spa, or the racquetball courts. And when I knocked on Ray's door, Ray was still half asleep, so he wasn't talking to his security man about our return trip.

After I'd exhausted every area of the hotel, I returned to the suite, and Silas let me in because I'd left without my key card. "Did you find him?"

I shook my head. "No."

Viktor shrugged as he poured himself a cup of coffee from the room service pot. "He'll come back. He's probably just bummed it's the last day." He paused and half smiled. "I know I am."

I nodded. "Me, too."

Silas raised his hand like we were taking some sort of school survey. "I'm joining the crowd."

Oh, how I was going to miss these guys. For the last two weeks, we had been joined at the hip. Having married them when I was seven in our "fake" ceremony that turned out to be very real was probably one of the best decisions I'd ever made.

I mean, of course, back then I hadn't known it would have to be undone legally for Henryk to take his place as King of Lichtenstein, and I certainly hadn't expected Silas and Viktor to blackmail Henryk into this vacation with us all. More than that though, I hadn't expected to want them all as much as I did.

Life was full of little surprises, or so I'd always heard anyway. Although, after this week in Ibiza with them and the sadness I was feeling at the thought of leaving them, I preferred my surprises to be less bittersweet than this one was turning out to be.

And just as if my thoughts had summoned more news, Silas's phone rang, and he walked to the charging station where he'd plugged it in the night before.

"It's Virginia."

I didn't know any Virginia, and didn't know how they knew a Virginia, but a little bubble of jealousy rolled into my belly.

"She's an admin back home in Seattle." Viktor smiled at me as if he knew what I was thinking. Or maybe he saw jealousy take its place in the form of my frown. It didn't matter, he'd cleared up the confusion.

Although, that she was calling meant nothing good for me.

"Hey, girl." Silas greeted her with a familiarity that made that little bubble grow. And then he put her on speaker and set the phone on the table in front of the sofa where I was sitting beside Viktor.

"Just got the word."

I checked the clock and tried to figure out the time difference. It was nine in the morning, Ibiza time. It had to be about midnight in Seattle. And it certainly sounded like there was some sort of celebration situation happening in the background. There was whooping and hollering and music.

The pause on her end was long enough that Viktor chimed in, "What word, Gin?"

"Gin?" I honestly didn't mean to say it aloud. Instead of calming my jealousy, he waved a hand in my face like he was trying to inflame it.

"Word that we got it. The development deal in Los Alamos!" she ended loudly, as if she were full fist-pumping behind the scenes.

"We got it?" Silas glanced at Viktor, who hadn't taken his eyes off the phone, although his mouth was hanging agape.

"Yeah, baby!" Viktor jumped up, pulled me up beside him then plastered a kiss against my mouth that was deep, hard and excited. When he pulled back, he gave his own fist pump. "Fuck, yeah, we did. You know why? Because we're the best out there!"

Silas took me by the arm and whipped me toward him, hugged me, swung me around off my feet, then kissed me as he set me down again. Their excitement was palpable, and I grinned until it hit me.

"You're going to New Mexico?" I asked, gulping hard. They had a new job, so any stupid ideas I had of us all being able to stay together were shattered. They had to go back. They wanted and needed this job. There were people counting on them. People whose livelihoods depended on this development deal. I couldn't get in the way of that. I wouldn't.

"Yeah, why not?" Silas grinned. "The money's great and the drinks are cheap!"

I let them celebrate, smiling anytime either of them looked at me, but inside, I was dying. I was going to lose them. Or Henryk. No way would I be lucky enough to have them all.

While they made their phone calls, I smiled when I needed to, and *celebrated* with them and the bottle of champagne Silas ordered from room service, and all the while, my heart was breaking for what was going to become of us.

I waited for Henryk to come back, and when he finally walked into the room, Silas and Viktor were on their phones still, so I walked to Henryk and threw myself against him, clinging to him, breathing in his scent, wishing I could freeze the moment with him because those, too, were coming to an end.

He lowered his head and kissed me softly, lingering when it ended, staring into my eyes. "I don't want to lose you, Erin."

His accent was the kind of thing dreams were made of. Mine, anyway. I couldn't imagine never hearing it again.

"I don't want to lose you either."

"When I saw you with them this morning, saw the passion, the connection…" He shook his head, looked away. "I can't ask you to stay with me."

"What if I want to?" I did, so badly.

"I have to marry Posey." His voice was soft, but the words were like a blade in my stomach. The pain welled inside me, making my stomach cramp. This wasn't the day we were all supposed to be having. Although, maybe it was. We'd all known that our time together was coming to an end. I don't think any of us expected us to feel so bad, though.

"I know." I shook my head. "But I can't be your mistress."

"Kings have long had mistresses." He said it softly as if it were actually an argument to try to convince me.

"Not me." And as hard as it was to do, I had to mean what I was saying. I had to make it clear. "I won't be your mistress." I walked away, out the door, and didn't stop walking until I was on the beach, staring at the waves rolling in on the sand.

# CHAPTER 2

## VIKTOR

As I watched Erin walk out, I sighed. This wouldn't be the end. We wouldn't let it be. But even if it was to be our last day together, I couldn't spend another fucking minute in this hotel room –pool or not, half-dressed Erin or not—watching them mope over having to head home. There wasn't anyone here who didn't know that eventually real life was going to come roaring back at us once this week was over. But if they didn't want to accept that instead of moping, they could've tried to come up with a solution.

Instead of spending this last day together, enjoying one another, these sad sacks were moping, their chins practically dragging the ground. I couldn't even stand to be in the same room.

I walked to the door across carpet so plush I sank with every step and yanked it open in a whoosh of air.

"Hey, where you going?" Silas called out, probably worried I was off to drown myself in the ocean. As if I were that kind of guy.

I didn't snap at him for being one of the mopers. I shrugged instead, and said, "I need some air."

The smell of fresh sea air and chemicals from the various pools mingled in the hallway. It was an odor I would always associate with this place. It was going to be the scent I would forever associate with Erin and this vacation.

Silas was probably in the room doubting my sanity or some other bullshit he would harass me about on the plane home. But he knew "air" was my catch-all excuse when I wanted to be left alone.

Certainly, he wouldn't buy it as an excuse now. It wasn't like we didn't have an open-air patio with a private pool and hot tub just outside the double French doors at the backside of the suite. But I needed air not filtered by their sadness.

Sometimes I didn't understand all this. How it happened. Why. We got "married" as a bunch of seven-year-olds when we were all in DC as children. We played at a park. Each of us—Henryk, Silas, and I— gave Erin a dandelion ring and proclaimed our undying love for one another after a few hours of afternoon play in a park. It was a child's game.

Then as an adult because he wanted to get married, Henryk told an off-handed story about a time in his life when he was happy as a child, and that was how we all ended up here in Ibiza, "celebrating" our divorce. But all this sadness was for the damned birds. It wasn't like any of us didn't know this moment would come.

Of course, that didn't mean that we were going to be happy about going our separate ways. There was real life to get back to. And we would all promise to stay in touch, not to wait another twenty years to see one another again, to call , write or visit. And we might, for a while. But eventually, life would intrude, and maybe someday we would look back, think about this weekend and how perfect it was. Maybe we would remember an incident or a perceived flaw, but this weekend would be the one that connected us more than the wedding that occurred when we were children.

The resort's main lobby was at the center of three off-shooting hallways. It was probably just the way I would've designed had I been in charge of building this place. It was central and required minimal staffing. Made sense from a business standpoint, and the aesthetic worked too.

There were two women manning the round counter. Another

woman ran a vacuum in the hallway. A couple walked through the sliding front door. Beside them was a valet with a luggage cart stacked with designer bags and suitcases. The woman wore a fur stole—in ninety-nine-degree weather—and shoes with pinpoint heels.

I walked toward the coffee shop, which was attached to the communal dining room where the hot breakfast buffet was served every morning. We hadn't ever eaten there because we always ordered room service. It was the prince's dime. We were using it to suit ourselves.

A girl with black hair and a wide smiled greeted in a British accent, "Good morning, sir."

"Good morning. Large black coffee…" I shook my head. "Scratch that. I want an iced caramel latte with oat milk." I'd tried Erin's yesterday and it was good. When she handed me my cup, I paid in cash, with American money because they took American currency here.

Hanging on one wall near the entrance to the resort's coffee shop was a display of pamphlets that touted things to do in Ibiza, excursions and day trips that could be booked through the hotel concierge.

That was when I saw the brochure. It was smaller than the others. Not as colorful, not as professionally made. But it was far more interesting than any of the others, to me anyway. And in big block letters, it said, *BOAT TO MARSEILLE.*

Now that was an idea I could get behind. It would extend our trip by a couple days, but we could all fly to our respective home bases from Marseille the same as we could back to Lichtenstein then home again.

All those years ago, when we'd "married" one another, I'd been so poor that half the nights I didn't have food in my belly. But, Erin , Henryk and Silas had treated me like I was every bit as good as they were. No one mentioned my torn shirt or the dirt on my face. We were just friends. Kids playing together at a playground. Where I'd come from hadn't mattered any more to them than where Henryk had come from mattered to me.

Once upon a time, we'd been the most important people in the world to each other. And these last few weeks, we were back there again. I didn't want to let it go yet.

I took the brochure—it was the only one in the case—and headed back to the suite. Of course, they were all still acting like their puppy had recently died when I walked in. The only one who bothered to look up was Erin, who must've decided the beach had little to offer on our last day. She smiled a little, soft and sad.

"All right." I picked up the remote and shut off the TV then turned to them. "I have an idea." I showed them the brochure, held it up like I was Vanna White, then handed it to Henryk. If he climbed on board, Silas and Erin would fall into place, too. I had hope.

Henryk looked at it and wrinkled his nose. "This boat isn't much."

"It has a cabin and captain." He handed the brochure to Erin. She stared at it silently, her face a mask of non-emotion. I wasn't ready to let it go. "Come on. It's gotta be better than flying. We can drink champagne on the deck." And three more days of Erin in a bikini wasn't such a bad selling point either.

Henryk looked at her, raised his eyebrows and asked the question without words. Sometimes his face said everything his words didn't, like now.

She looked from Henryk to Silas and then to me. "I like it." Her smile broadened and her eyes sparkled. "I'm not ready to say goodbye yet."

I wasn't either. I looked at Silas, who nodded then shrugged. "I wouldn't mind taking a boat back."

Henryk smiled. "All right then, let's do it." He took the pamphlet and pulled out his phone to call Ray. "I'll get it set up."

He walked toward the bedroom, then stopped and turned back to us. "Ray says the security is too difficult to manage on the open water."

I shrugged, not feeling at all charitable, and I didn't give a fuck what Ray had to say about it. I wanted this, and I wasn't going to let Fancy Pants take it from me. "Then fly back and we'll see you at the castle." I said it with a smile. No way in hell would that ever be an option, and he didn't have to say it for us to all know it. If the rest of us were on the boat, he would be too.

Erin hadn't said much yet, and I glanced at her. She was watching the prince, her hand on his arm. "We should go, Henryk. It could be our last chance to be together." The sadness on her face was his fault because he couldn't stand up to his family and his country and claim the life he wanted over the one he had been born into. I couldn't blame him, but I wasn't sure I could forgive him for doing this to her and, by extension, to us, either.

"Ray won't like it." He was wavering. There was no real strength in his refusal.

"Probably not." Erin was smiling because she had him now, and there wasn't a person in the room, including Henryk, who didn't know it.

He took the brochure and looked at it again. "I'll have Ray set it up."

"Negative." I shook my head. "I'll handle it." My party, my rules, and Fancy Pants can learn to like it.

He handed over the piece of paper and stared at me like I was step-ping on his toes, but I didn't give a fuck. For once, we were doing something my way. "Fine. Book the boat."

It was going to take every dime I had in savings, but I wasn't worried. We had the big Los Alamos job, and it was going to bring a shit ton more work. We were getting the crew, the jet skis and the next few days alone. And that alone was worth whatever that all cost.

# CHAPTER 3

## HENRYK

The boat wasn't nearly as grand or as extravagant as the brochure claimed. There were barnacles and long black smudges where the side had rubbed against a dock. Certainly, it wasn't a yacht. It was more a long boat with a couple cabins. There was a dining room attached to a small galley, but the deck was wide and impressive. and I stood at the rail looking at the coast of Ibiza as it became smaller and smaller.

I felt her coming before I turned to see her. Sometimes seeing her knocked me so far out of my comfort zone, I hardly remembered to breathe. She was the most beautiful woman I'd ever laid eyes on. If I were honest, I hadn't ever forgotten her, not since we were kids in the park playing that day.

When I'd returned to the embassy that night and told my mother about her, I'd been upset that I was leaving, and would never see my new friends again. But really, it was Erin I'd wanted to see, Erin I'd wanted to bring home to the castle in Lichtenstein with me. I cried like my heart was broken –because it was—when my father told me it wasn't possible. My mother had pacified me with the promise of a return trip, but when I returned to DC, to the park there, I'd been older, and if Erin had been there, I certainly would have seen her. I hadn't gone back after.

Strangely, that time felt as if it had only just happened. I remembered the feel of the sun on my face, the way her hand fit in mine, the smell of the flowers beside the playground and the way they grew up a concrete wall, spreading their scent with every slight blow of the wind.

And here we all were, together again.

Silas was standing at the rail beside Erin on one side, and she had Viktor on the other. I was separate from them, as always. Even when we were all together, loving her, I didn't know that I was the one who belonged, but I didn't feel as out of place as I did in this moment, one that seemed private between them.

When she tilted her chin up and smiled at Silas, she was so beautiful. Especially with the water as a backdrop, reflecting the sunlight on her. It was a funny trick of light, but she appeared to have a halo shining over her head. The effect was an optical illusion, but it made me want her.

Hell, if I were to tell the truth, everything made me want her. She was sensual and sexy and a woman who knew what she wanted. There was nothing more attractive than that. On every level. Forthright and honest about her desires regarding how she wanted to be pleased. It was intoxicating.

The sea was gentle, and the boat sliced a path away from the shore, leaving a white-capped wake behind. Sea sprayed behind but not onto the boat.

There were windows to the engine room at the front of the boat. The captain was a big man with a wiry beard and hair gathered in the back to a bun. It was a very Caribbean look –complete with a shell necklace--and I smiled because I trusted a man sailing me away who had a bun. Of all the sentences I thought I would say in my life, that certainly wasn't one of them.

He gave a wave, and I turned back to observing the others watching the ocean pass by. My back to the water, watching them all smile and laugh, I wished I knew how to join them. How to walk up and insert myself into their conversation, into their friendship. But I was awkward. As a prince, a man who had met literally thousands of people in his life, I didn't have the skills to join them without making myself into the odd man out. It was a rather sobering and depressing thought.

I walked to the cabin below and poured myself a glass of wine. Prior to our arrival, the boat had been stocked with red and white, canned meats and pasta. Two kinds of beer. Funnily enough, I hadn't seen a life jacket or raft since we boarded. But I wasn't worried. The Caribbean captain with the bun would never dare wreck our boat. I had every confidence.

The crew had their own cabin below the deck. I didn't know where it was in relation to ours, but I wondered as we stood here together and apart, if we would need to worry about any of this appearing in a tabloid. Thanks to my brother, Nicky, I trusted no one these days.

I laughed to myself. Darling Nicky. My mother's favorite son. Not my father's. Or maybe my father's, not my mother's. It was often difficult to tell from day to day. Nicky had the luxury of privacy, a life not followed by the long lenses of paparazzi reporters. I'd not had such a luxury since childhood. Probably that day in DC was the only one. I'd left as an ordinary boy.

Not coincidentally, it was also the last time until we were all together again that I could ever remember being happy, not duty-bound.

I had but a few days of this freedom left, and I didn't want to spend it below the deck, hiding from the people I had come to trust and need in my life. I pulled two beers from the chest and poured a second glass of wine. I tucked the beers under my arm, picked up the wines, then walked carefully up the steps from below. The sea spray was a light mist, and I smiled. They were laughing.

I joined in because it didn't feel awkward, and then I handed the drinks around to them. Silas nodded his head. "You must have a sixth sense, bro." He clinked his bottle against my glass and smiled as he tipped the beer back and took a deep pull.

"Right on," Viktor quipped.

But it was Erin who took her glass from me and smiled, laid her hand on my chest and raised on her tiptoes to kiss my cheek. "Very thoughtful, Henryk."

My cheeks flushed with heat. I loved hearing her say my name. "I was thirsty." I shrugged as if it was no big deal. But the truth was, it was usually Ray who was the thoughtful one, who handled refreshments for my guests before I ever thought of it.

Silas turned back to the water and pointed out a pod of dolphins to Viktor, and I would have looked but I couldn't take my eyes off Erin. Plus, I'd seen my share of dolphins. This wasn't my first trip across the ocean.

Erin cupped my cheek with her palm and guided my face so I was looking down at her. I loved being touched by her, looking into her eyes, seeing her smile. Loved that she was giving me this amount of attention individually.

"There are many layers to you." I didn't know what she meant.

"Because I brought drinks?" I was curious as to what she meant. What layers she could see that I couldn't?

"Because you're gentle and fierce. Kind and embattled."

"Embattled?" I didn't know that I liked the sound of that, or the connotation.

"Embattled by your duty to the crown." She spoke softly and moved closer to me so that her body was pressed closer to mine. "Sexy and reserved."

"Less reserved since I met you." I very much enjoyed having her pressed against me. Her body fit against mine in a way no woman ever had before. Not that there were many women allowed so close. The vetting process was too stringent for most.

"You, my prince, are a conundrum."

I didn't care about anything other than she called me *her* prince. Whether she knew it or was merely teasing, I was hers. A hundred percent hers. Always hers.

Her hand slid from my face, down my throat to rest over my heart.

"You're going to make a very good king." Her smile was bittersweet. "Posey is very lucky."

"I don't want to think about Posey right now." These few days we had left were a gift, and I didn't want to waste them.

I wanted to think of Erin, to celebrate her beauty with kisses along her skin. I wasn't then, nor had I ever been a poetic man, and to be honest, I had little respect for those who were. But she inspired me to want to be more, to want to romance her in ways I never had to be with a woman.

Her kiss was slow and soft, but sensual. Sexy. I felt it all the way to my soul.

"We should get ready for dinner," she said when she finally pulled back.

I nodded, although I would have gladly starved for more time in her arms. Well, not starved, but fasted for a few hours. I smiled at the thought.

The captain came out of the engine room and nodded. "Would you all like to eat on the deck this evening or below deck?"

"The deck is fine," Viktor said, with grit in his tone. This was his trip, and he obviously didn't want to be ignored when decisions were to be made.

The captain nodded much the same way my father's valet did when he left the room. The captain backed toward his engine room and picked up his two-way radio. I assumed that was so he could speak to his crew. I didn't really care. What I cared about was that Erin had moved away, gone below deck.

The sun was about to set, and the sky was a thousand shades of red and orange and I wanted to share it with her, but she'd left so I stared at it, pulling out my cell if for no other reason than I wanted to remember this day.

I glanced at the corner of the phone where NO SERVICE was displayed. We were too far from land. That was okay. I could definitely do without my mother's incessant complaining about my late return, so it was not a task to ignore the uneasiness of being cut off from the world. Likely, this would be my last chance for such a thing.

The crew worked to set a table on the deck, covered it with a crisp white linen cloth then set a candle lantern in the center. A bottle of wine with four glasses and a shined stainless-steel cooler sat to one side with an assortment of other drinks.

Being in the center of the ocean was disorienting now that I could no longer see land. I had no bearings on the direction of our travel, and it would be worse when the sun set. It was unsettling in ways I'd never encountered.

As soon as the table was set, we all sat, but then Erin stood and ran for the cabin steps. She disappeared below, and I poured us each a glass of wine. I didn't pour for Viktor or Silas because they were already drinking beer.

We didn't toast or even speak much. There wasn't anyone on this boat who didn't know we were only prolonging the inevitable, but I was happy, for now anyway, to pretend that it wasn't going to end at all.

Erin returned after a few minutes, holding one long box and two smaller ones. Each was gift wrapped and tied with a bow. She handed me the long box and set one in front of each of the others.

Shit. I should've thought to get gifts. These people had come to mean something to me, and a token to show my appreciation would not have been out of line.

I stared for a second until she nudged me. "Open them." As Silas, Viktor and I pulled the ribbons, Erin smiled, holding her hands clasped in front of her mouth as if she was trying not to blurt out whatever was on her mind. I was the first to separate the paper and open the flap on the long, slender white box. I pulled the pieces of tissue paper open. "Oh, Erin."

It was long and slender, and I knew immediately what it was. A telescope. I pulled it out of the box, and she moved the wrapper and ribbon away so I could keep both hands around it as I put it to my eye and looked out at the water.

"I feel like a real sailor," I said, smiling. "This is beautiful."

"I thought that if we're apart, at night you could go outside, see the stars and know I was looking up at the same ones in the same sky." She smiled softly as though she knew the thoughts that had been eating my soul all day.

I leaned over and kissed her soundly. She was beautiful and sweet and thoughtful. She deserved the world.

When I sat back, Viktor had an antique compass in his hand. He smiled at her. "I have a collection of these back home."

She nodded. "I know. Silas told me. And I found this one when we were out shopping in Ibiza." She motioned to the compass as Silas opened his box containing a long, hilted knife in a sheath. "And Viktor told me you like to hunt." She was proud of her purchases. Her face was aglow with color and happiness, and she was always exquisite but was so much more so when she was happy.

Dinner was ripe with conversation. We discussed the weather, the boat, the gifts, how happy we all were that we decided to do this.

After dinner, when the crew took the table away, we played soft music on an old radio and danced on the deck, all together. Erin divided her time evenly, but I wanted all her attention. I wanted her hands on me. I wanted her eyes locked on mine.

Silas drew her close, whirled her out then back in, sashayed her in a small circle, then she spun away and into Viktor's chest. He tilted her chin up in a Swayze move I didn't know anyone else could have ever pulled off. But he made look suave and effortless. I could do the same thing a hundred times, and not much chance anyone would ever call me suave or effortless.

Finally, she worked her way around back to me, and I held her close to me, pressed a kiss to her cheek, and smiled when I pulled back. There was no experience that compared holding her, unless it was kissing her and all that it led to… was leading to. She had that sparkle in her eye.

I smiled at her. She was so beautiful, I knew in that moment I would never want another woman more than I wanted her.

She tugged my hand toward the steps that led below to the cabin and the bed. I didn't care if the others followed. I cared even less when she tugged my shirt over my head and pressed a kiss against my heart.

Later, when I was married to Posey, I would only have these memories to see me through, because Erin had made it clear, and I agreed that I wouldn't want her to lower her standards of morality for me, that there was no way we would be doing this once I was married.

She wound her arms around my neck and curled her fingers into my hair, pulling me down to sear my lips with hers. It was the most erotic kiss I'd ever tasted. The most sensual. I unfastened her shirt and slid it from her shoulders as Silas and Viktor came down the steps.

Viktor growled because he was a man who didn't use a lot of words to convey his emotions, but Silas smiled and nodded at Erin. "Oh, yeah."

Erin spun to face Silas and kissed him, then kissed Viktor as she unfastened Silas's belt. He was wearing khaki shorts and a thin black belt that Erin flung behind her. I ducked out of the way of the buckle as it sailed past my head. Then she started fumbling with the button.

I was a lucky man. We all were because she was exquisite and sexy. Sensual.

Her mouth was hot by the time she came back around to me. Her hands were like fire on my skin. And she pulled me down again, this time as she backed toward the bed. I crawled over so my body covered her while she backed onto the mattress.

Every inch I moved brought me closer to being inside her. I would've moved the world for that.

She pulled Silas in for a kiss, and I watched her mouth work his, the expertise and passion that mixed together to make him moan from deep in his chest. And when she kissed Viktor and he moaned, I could have moaned with him.

But then she kissed me, and I moved to the side of her that Silas vacated. He took the spot between her legs and shimmied her shorts down her legs, over her feet. She was naked and glorious. I wanted to touch all of her, but I settled for one beautiful breast, a hard nipple I flicked with my tongue while Viktor ran his hand across her belly and kissed her.

As Viktor and I switched positions and I took the kisses while he teased her nipples, Silas licked her clit. She writhed but there was nowhere for her to go. She turned her head to look at me with deliciously half-lidded eyes and parted lips.

"I want you in my mouth." Her voice was little more than a whisper, and I was certainly going to oblige. I shifted out of the swim trunks I was still wearing and moved into position as she licked her lips and stared at the bead of precum on the head of my cock.

As soon as her mouth wrapped around my dick, my head fell back, and I breathed out a stuttering exhale. She moaned, and the vibration was almost more than I could take. She licked and sucked and swirled her tongue until I was groaning. She worked her free hand over Viktor's cock, and he watched her as she gave and took, and then he clenched his hands in the pillow beside her head and shot cum on her chest as she writhed and cried out around my cock. It was enough to draw the orgasm from my body in shudders and guttural moans.

And then Silas moved between her legs, and I watched as he pumped in and out of her. It wasn't long before Silas's head fell back and he groaned, shuddered and stilled.

I closed my eyes, savoring every second, every breath. Once I was married to Posey this was all over. And I wasn't even close to ready to let it all end.

# CHAPTER 4

## SILAS

It would have been easy to get used to all of this, to living on a boat and sleeping beside Erin every night. She spread her time between us evenly, and she made sure no one was left out. The result was pure magic.

We spent the next day on the deck, and the captain dropped the anchor for a while. I couldn't see land anymore, which I thought was odd. I was pretty sure we were supposed to stay near the shoreline.

We were going to take the jet skis out later, but we spent the morning swimming and diving off the boat. We were having fun as if we didn't have a care in the world. I wished that were the case, but Vik and I needed to get back to Seattle to get materials ordered, sub-contractors lined up. The job was in New Mexico, so that was going to require accommodations and a lot more stuffing around than we were used to.We'd bid on this project too low. I'd tried to tell him, but he'd just assured me in his calm and confident Viktor way that it was all going to be okay. We could work it out.

I wanted to believe him. So much. But worry gnawed in my gut. I didn't know if we even knew enough sub-contractors for all the jobs we had coming in. If I were honest, we didn't have time for this extra trip, and certainly didn't have time to be anchored and swimming.

But since we were here, and it didn't look as if we were moving anytime soon, there wasn't much point in fretting. I forcibly pushed the thoughts out of my mind and watched as Erin dove off the side of the boat into the water.

She had good form. And the fact that she'd chosen her skimpiest bikini didn't hurt one bit. She was tanned, toned and graceful. It definitely wasn't a hardship to look at her.

Henryk was in the water with her, and I could imagine that for him, this trip must have been a relief. It must have been nice not to have to worry about reporters watching him, drones taking pictures, people knowing what time of day he took a dump. This was probably as private as the prince ever managed to get.

When I looked out again, I couldn't see land or any trace of it. There should've been something. A shadow of land. An outline of a city. But all I could see on all four sides was water. So much water. I didn't know then what the opposite of claustrophobia was, but suddenly, I had it.

There was too much open space. I had a tightness in my chest and a gnawing in my gut. I couldn't catch a breath.

I couldn't be sure who was talking to me, but Viktor helped me to a chair, and I sat, heavy and hard. "We should be able to see land."

"I'm sure we're just out to sea for a moment." His voice, with its sometimes gruff accent, was soft now. "You have to breathe, Silas."

I pulled as much air into my chest as I could manage, held it for a solid five count, then blew it out. But even then, I didn't get any relief. The world was spinning. We were too far out. We should've been near the coastline. Certainly, it was what we'd all talked about, stopping at cities and ports on the coast.

"Where is. The land?" They were the only words I could manage. I couldn't speak more than that. And I couldn't stand the idea that we were in a position of helplessness. It burned through me, the feeling of being at someone else's mercy, the weakness of it.

"It's probably just over there." He pointed in the direction I thought was more out to sea than we already were. Then he turned.

"Or maybe it's over there." He motioned to the other side of the yacht. "I'm sure the captain knows."

My mind worked differently. I could give people the benefit of the doubt, but I'd lost confidence in what Viktor was saying now.

I stared out at the horizon, turned to look at the other horizon line. Spun to see two more. I couldn't tell where I was. Being out to sea and in the middle of the ocean was disorienting. Made my stomach curl.

Viktor looked, too.

I reeled the panic in, pulling myself together. Mostly. "You got a compass from Erin."

Viktor nodded. "Yeah, but I don't know if it works."

It was worth a try. He left me for a moment to go to the cabin but returned. We should have been traveling north, or some manner of north. But I was almost sure we were going south.

He returned with the compass, flicked it open, and he stood waiting for a definitive answer. "We're going southeast." Then he turned and turned and turned again. "Southeast."

That was wrong. Marseille was north of Ibiza. Another flare of panic burst into my gut.

Erin climbed back on the boat at the spot where the jet skis launched. The jet skis, however, were not there.

She waved us down from the deck. "You guys are missing all the fun."

Right now, she could frolic all she wanted with the prince. I didn't want to alarm her. Instead, I was going to go see the captain. But whatever she saw in my face worried her, so she wrapped herself in a towel then climbed up to stand beside Vik. A few seconds later, Henryk followed so that we were all on the deck. I looked back and upward at the bridge. On a normal day, I could see the captain. On a normal day, he was charting, watching the water, checking the sky, and whatever other things a captain did on a yacht. Today, I couldn't see him. My guts were twisted tight now.

I didn't look too hard because I didn't want the others to see—or not see—what I was thinking. I didn't want to sound the alarm. I also didn't want to panic or cause the others any unnecessary worry. But I needed the captain. There had to be an explanation why we were so far from land.

I looked over the side of the yacht for the small boat that had been there since we set off from Ibiza. It was gone. So now, there was no rescue boat, no jet skis and no captain. It might have been time to panic after all.

I looked at the others. Right now, no one was troubled, no one was unhappy. I wanted them to hold those feelings for a while longer, so I smiled at Erin, gave her a little wink, then said, "I'll be back in a few minutes."

As calmly as if I hadn't a care in the world, I went to the bridge and pushed the door open. It was empty, of course. The radio was destroyed. Gauges were smashed. On the counter beside the throttle handle that was also deformed, badly misshapen, obviously damaged, was a two-way radio.

"Hello?" I spoke into the bottom of the radio. "This is the boat Enchantment. Is anyone listening?"

A voice came back. "Go ahead, Enchantment."

"We are at sea. Our instrument panels have been destroyed and we are off course. I can't find our captain or our crew. Please say you can do some voodoo kind of magic, find us, and tow us to shore." It didn't hurt to ask.

The voice on the other end of the radio laughed. "This is Captain Donatello." Oh, shit. "There is enough food on the boat and enough water for a couple of days. As you've probably guessed, the boat is immobile, so you're going to have to wait for water rescue to find you."

If I ever got my hands on this guy, I was going to put an end to him in ways that made his guts wish they were on the outside of his body. "You son of a bitch."

"As soon as the ransom is paid, we'll tell the authorities where to find the boat, and you will be rescued." A tint of deep maroon colored my vision. I was going to kill this fuck. "For now, you should enjoy your time together with the prince and the woman."

"Send someone for us. *Now.*" I put anger and rage into my tone but couldn't very well back it up. I was stuck on a boat in the middle of the fucking ocean with no way to get to dry land.

This wasn't a sailboat and even if it was, none of us were sailors. I was certain the engines were toast. Two fucking engines, neither one worth a damn. Didn't that figure.

I walked out onto the deck and let the door slam behind me. They all looked up at me and I shook my head at Vik. He knew. The others didn't. Yet. And someone had to tell them.

When I walked down the stairs and came to stand beside Erin, she laid her hand on my chest. "What is it?"

I had to tell them, but hell... what a job. "We've been hijacked or maybe more accurately, abandoned."

Erin's gaze flipped up to meet mine, while Henryk turned away on a curse.

Vik shook his head. "How do you know?"

I held up the radio. "Captain still had his on. Said as soon as the ransom is paid, he'll tell them how to find us and we'll be rescued." There wasn't much else I could say. It was all I knew. All that mattered.

Henryk turned around and muttered, "That isn't our biggest problem."

I wanted to throttle him. I was almost certain he was going to say we had better hope for a quick rescue because his mother or his father or his national fucking guard was going to take it badly that we were in the middle of the ocean instead of Marseille as we promised.

I sighed because my stomach ached. I wasn't in the mood for his fancy pants whining. "What, your highness? What the fuck is our biggest problem if it isn't being stuck on a boat with enough food and water for three or four days?"

He turned to me and shook his head, pointed to the sky and the line of black clouds moving in closer to us with each tiny little wave that lapped against the boat. "That. That is our biggest problem."

The wind came first, blowing with enough intensity to almost lay the yacht on its side. A hundred and fifty feet of boat. We held on, waiting for the end to come, for the ocean to overtake the vessel. I'd never been so terrified in all my life.

Each of us wore a life jacket and tried to battle the shifts and jerks, but it was like being tossed around in a washing machine.

Erin screamed, I gulped, and Viktor shook his head when the anchor line snapped, and the boat went adrift. We were already off our planned course. Already unlikely to be found easily. The odds were not in our favor now.

Cabinets opened and the things inside went crashing down. At one point, the boat tilted enough, it pulled Erin's feet from beneath her.

By the time the rain came, Henryk was bleeding, Erin was frantic, and Viktor was injured. And then the water—more than the rain from above—started coming into the cabin. We were taking on water.

I didn't know whether we were safer on the boat or off it. I couldn't imagine that either was a very good option, considering we hadn't been through the worst of it yet.

# CHAPTER 5

## ERIN

*Day One*

It wasn't the pain that woke me, or the wind still blowing like a banshee, or even the fact that I was half in water and half on sand. It wasn't the fact that I had to pee—which I did. It was the fact that my foot was cold. So fucking cold I thought it might freeze off. But that was because it was dunked in the water and the cold rain was still falling.

I sat up and pulled my aching leg out of the water, crawled up the sand while rain pelted me in the face. Each drop was like a little needle against my skin. I forced my eyes open and desperately looked for shelter. There was none. And that begged the question… where were we?

While I didn't know where we'd landed, I was certainly never going to forget how we got here. I was going to have nightmares about last night. The boat tipping and cracking as the waves hit us over and over. The crumbling of wood around us, the scream of twisting metal. And I was going to remember last night and the horror of it all for as long as I lived.

How we got here, assuming we'd all arrived—and I prayed we did

—didn't matter so much right now as making sure we were all alive. I looked left and saw sand, looked right and there was even more sand. Then an incline and a cliff with water crashing against the rocks beneath. What I didn't see was Henryk, Silas or Viktor. I was alone.

The shakes came first. My whole body was vibrating with fear. I was going to die here, in the middle of nowhere, alone. The tears started, and pain overwhelmed me. I was done for.

A moment before I opened my mouth to scream, I looked up and there was Henryk. He had a line of blood streaming from the top of his head, down his cheek, but he was walking—staggering might be more accurate—toward me, kicking sand, one shoe on, one missing. But he was walking. And alive.

He saw me and moved quicker, dragging one leg behind him, but he was still upright. His knee wasn't bending on the leg he was dragging though, and my heart broke to see him hurt. I crawled towards him, unable to get to my feet.

When he got to me, he grabbed me under the arms and hauled me to my feet with a groan. I woodenly fell against him and cried softly into his shoulder, relief at finding him hitting me harder than the rain.

I held on tightly because there had been a long moment when I woke up that I thought I might die or perhaps be dead. And I'd never been so afraid in all my life. I needed this hug more than anything else in the world.

Then it occurred to me that Henryk was alone. I lifted my head and gasped out, "Where's Viktor? And Silas?" My hands trembled as I pulled back and began to frantically spin in search of them. My gaze raked over the beach and the tall grass behind us. There was a cliff and some water, more rain, and then I saw it. A piece of the boat washed up farther down the beach. I thought it was the front, but I wouldn't have known the difference.

I broke out of Henryk's embrace, "Oh my God. I see the boat."

I took off running –stumbling—to the busted hull. "Viktor! Silas!" I called out their names as I ran, my lungs burning.

There was nothing. No one called out, and I couldn't see hide nor hair of my men. I'd run up and down the beach but not around to the cliff side. No way would they have been able to get up there.

I screamed out their names until I was hoarse. It wasn't until I leaned against a piece of the boat lying on its side on the sand, sobbing uncontrollably, that I heard someone calling out. "Erin! Henryk! Silas!"

I wiped my eyes and stared towards the sound. Viktor was walking toward me, apparently uninjured as far as I could see. He was upright, not bloody, and nothing was dragging behind. I ran to him and hugged him so tightly my arms ached.

He pulled back but didn't let go of me as he stared. "Are you all right? Are you hurt?"

"I'm fine," I said, wiping at the tears on my cheeks. "Are you?"

"A little sore, banged up a bit, but I think I'm okay." When Henryk walked over, Vik pulled him in for a hug too. "Where's Silas?" There was an edge to his voice, and I looked down.

I didn't know, and it was killing me. I shook my head.

Viktor cupped his hands around his mouth and shouted, "Silas!" over and over again as he walked toward the part of beach where I'd been. "We have to find him."

He looked at Henryk and me. There weren't a lot of places to hide. Unless there was something on the other side of that cliff formation, he had to be around here. He just had to.

"Let's split up," I said, with a confidence I didn't feel. "He has to be here."

I walked into the tall grass, glad I'd changed from my swimming suit to jeans on the boat, even though they were soaked and only getting wetter from the rain. "Silas?" I tried to walk in some semblance of a grid, but I was disoriented and couldn't seem to focus on more than calling out his name.

My heart raced and my stomach clenched. No one knew where we were, and one of us was missing. This place would've been kind of beautiful if we hadn't been forced here by the storm and our ship-wreck. We were trapped in paradise.

There were palm trees around us and at least one banana tree.

There was also a lot of beach, and the cliffs that jutted out over the water. Tall grass led inland, but I didn't want to tempt fate by walking too far into it. Who knew what lived in there.

I took a deep breath. I didn't have much of a choice. We had to find Silas.

Henryk limped toward the cliff and started the trek up. He was working his leg, stopping to bend it after every few steps. His wince of pain was obvious, but I couldn't feel sorry about that right now. We had to find Silas, then we could assess injuries. He made it to the top of the cliff as I was about halfway through the patch of grass on our side of the place. He looked out at the water. "I see him!" He pointed toward the ocean.

I started rushing back through the grass, but I was ages from the water. Viktor jumped in the ocean and took off swimming in the direction Henryk was pointing.

"I got him!" he called out, then added, "I need help."

I waded out, the water freezing and making my skin scream in anger. Viktor was tugging Silas on his back towards me on some sort of raft. Wood from the wreckage, probably.

Silas was neither small nor light, and the water in his clothes would have made him heavier. But he was alive. Unconscious and alive, bleeding from a head wound with his leg twisted at a bad angle, but breathing.

"Got him!" I called out when they reached us, and I helped Viktor drag him to the beach and laid him near the edge of the grass. "Is he breathing?" Henryk asked.

I dropped to my knees beside him and put my hands on his chest. "Yeah." I didn't know what to do to wake up him up or even if it was safe to try. Instead, I brushed his hair back off his forehead and gave him a little shake. Vik took one of the life jackets – his or mine, I didn't know which—and put it under Silas's head. "We need a first aid kit."

Vik looked out at the water. "The other part of the boat is right there." He pointed to the water. "See it?"

I squinted toward where he was pointing. I hadn't noticed it before. "Oh."

Maybe there were things we could salvage from the boat. Like clothes to stay warm or bottles of water. The first aid kit, definitely. And now that I knew the boat was there, I couldn't stop seeing it, or watching the water slosh against it as the waves rolled in. I wanted to swim out and see if there was anything out there that could help us or Silas.

"They're going to find us, right?" I just needed one of them to say it, then I would be fine. I trusted these guys. I wasn't immature enough to think that just because they said something, it would become reality, but the reassurance was enough for me.

Henryk nodded, and Vik smiled. "You bet. We'll probably be picked up before the sun sets tonight." When I glanced at Silas, though, my chest squeezed with worry.

I hoped so because there was only so much nature and roughing it a girl could take, and I was at my limit.

I glanced at Silas and waited, closed my eyes and tried to will him my life force, my energy, my ability to open my eyes. I just needed to make sure he was okay. I pulled one of his eyelids up and stared. Then I let it close and looked at the other.

"What are you doing, Erin?" Viktor asked and held his hand up like he was ready to swat my hands away.

"I don't know, but when someone is passed out on TV, Dr. Shepard pulls up an eyelid and looks." I shrugged. It made sense to me.

"Does the person usually wake up?" Henryk rejoined us.

I could see neither one of these two watched many TV medical dramas. "Sometimes, but then they always rush them into a CT scan or to surgery." I sighed. Not much I wouldn't do for a Dr. Shepard of our own right now and his CT machine, so he could save Silas. Sadly, that wasn't a realistic option for us or anyone, but it was a fun thought.

Fun thoughts weren't going to wake Silas however, and I needed Silas to wake up and I needed him to do it now.

My heart was pounding, and I felt useless. I didn't know anything. Tears streamed down my cheeks, and I wiped them away.

I wasn't a particularly religious person, but I wished I was. I wanted to pray, to have faith in some higher power who could help us right now. Silas needed medical attention, and we were in the middle of the fucking ocean.

"Hey." His voice was weak. "Don't cry."

I sucked in a breath. He was awake. "Oh, Silas!" I leaned down, took his face in my hands and kissed his cheeks and his forehead, which had a bump that was scraped raw, and I avoided it. "You're awake."

"Mm-hmm." But then his eyes closed again, and he stopped speaking.

I closed my eyes and willed him awake again, but nothing happened.

# CHAPTER 6

## HENRYK

The island was smaller than I first assumed. The concept of islands had always fascinated me much more than being on one. I'd often wondered what kept them anchored when all around them was nothing but water. What stopped one from floating away until it collided with another land mass? I'd never in my wildest dreams imagined I would be stranded on one. But here I was. Here we all were.

No food. No phone service. No shelter.

I was standing in the water, a foot or so from dry land, stomach churning as I waited for Erin to return from her swim out to the boat. She'd insisted that she be the one to go. Viktor was standing vigil over Silas, watching him for any sign he might wake soon.

These were my friends now, and I cared deeply about them all. Silas had to wake up, or none of us would be the same. Erin had been gone for too long now. I'd promised to give her time before I followed her out. She'd spoken passionately about air pockets and the like. I'd ignored her just as passionately. Refused to let her go. But she'd insisted and she'd won.

I didn't have a watch to see the exact number of minutes and seconds she'd been underwater, but it was a lot longer than I was comfortable with. My heart was pounding harder, thumping against my ribs now. I took a step deeper into the ocean, ready to swim out despite the fact she was a much better swimmer than me. Then she popped up out of the water, and my breath rushed out of me in a sigh of relief. She stood up and waded out of the ocean, emerging like a warrior woman. She had a bag slung over her back and a bottle of champagne in her hand.

"I got some food, some drinks and the first aid kit."

"You were gone forever." I didn't care about the stuff she'd managed to get her hands on. I only cared that she was okay.

"I found an air pocket. I told you there was one." She was so excited to have succeeded I tried not to say anything negative. There was a glow to her cheeks and a bounce in her step as she danced across the sand. "We have food!"

She pulled out some fresh fruit—a cantaloupe, some bananas and a couple of bunches of grapes that had traveled well—and laid them on the sand with a jar of salsa, some chips that were unopened and looked crisp. Some oysters. "I didn't trust anything in the fridge. Except that." She pointed to the food on the beach then started taking more things out of her pack. "Champagne, wine, a bottle of vodka. The first aid kit. Your telescope, Silas's knife. I can go back in a minute for some fishing rods."

Her excitement rang through every sentence, every syllable. She was bouncing, she was so excited. And in all this ridiculousness— abandoned for ransom and then stranded—she was a light in the darkness. As beautiful, certainly, as the landscape and the crystal-clear water near the beach.

"You should rest for a minute." I didn't want to dampen her excite- ment, especially since she was so radiant with it, but I also didn't want her to over-exert herself either. We'd already been through enough trauma already. "Or for a while."

She grinned up at me. "I don't need a rest."

"Erin..."

"Henryk, you're the prince of Lichtenstein. No way is someone not searching for us right now. Viktor, Silas and I are American citizens. They're going to look for us, and they're going to find us."

I loved her enthusiasm. It was refreshing since I'd been thinking the opposite. I'd been thinking that my brother, the ever jealous and too young to be king, Nikolai, would never let a ransom demand through to my parents. Therefore, the only way anyone had a chance of delivering a message was if they took it to Ray.

Hopefully, that was what they did. I'd also been worrying about the fact that no one really knew where we'd gone, even our kidnappers.

Erin moved to sit beside me as if she knew what I was thinking. "Do you know that I never learned to play chess? I can play checkers. I can kick your ass at Monopoly, at Sorry and Scrabble and cornhole, but I can't play chess."

I didn't know what I was supposed to say to that. "Oh."

She smiled and nodded. "So I have to get off the island so some-one…" She paused and brushed her fingers down my cheek and my eyes closed on a wave of happiness. "You… hopefully, can teach me to play chess. No one who wants to learn to play chess dies on an island without learning how."

"You know that for a fact?"

She grinned, and it was the best thing I'd seen in a long time. "Yeah. I've done the research."

"I'm glad."

Viktor watched us for a minute then stood and walked over. "You're back."

"I am." She turned that grin toward him, and I wanted more minutes alone with her. "And I brought goodies." When she held up the champagne, she giggled. Silas was only a few feet away, so it wasn't as if he was in any more danger than if we were beside him.

Viktor looked at the telescope and at Silas's knife. "Good. We can use these things."

"I couldn't find your compass." She sounded sad, her voice softer and deeper than a second ago.

"I have it." He reached into his pocket and pulled it out. It looked more like a pocket watch than a compass, but he was proud of it, proud enough to keep it in his pocket. Her eyes glittered when she laid her hand over it where it sat in his palm.

And then she rose onto her tiptoes and kissed him in a less than chaste manner. His arm wrapped around her waist and pulled her closer as I watched them.

The kiss, which at first didn't look like it was going to be much, turned sensual, and his hands slipped from her waist to her ass. I hadn't done much watching lately, but I was oddly aroused seeing the way he touched her, the way they touched each other. She pushed his shirt up and flung it off and he returned the favor so that there were miles of her luscious skin exposed. My fingers tingled for a touch.

He stopped kissing her mouth and went lower to take a perfect pert nipple between his teeth. My balls tightened and I knelt in the sand, watching, close enough I could see everything, and it was glorious. Her skin glistened with a sheen of sweat, and my mouth watered for a taste, but more than that, I wanted to watch her.

Viktor turned her toward me, and she reached an arm up to wind around his neck as he kissed her from her shoulder to the side of her throat. His hands remained on her breasts, tweaking and squeezing her nipples, kneading the soft flesh around them.

Oh, God. This was live-action porn of the sensual and sexy kind. My cock throbbed and I unfastened my pants, almost afraid if I touched it, it would explode, but need and desire were stronger. I curled my fingers around the shaft and stroked slowly, firmly.

She ground her ass against his groin, and he moaned then stripped out of his pants, bent his knees around hers and plunged inside of her with an upward thrust. She cried out and reached for me. "Please, Henryk."

She didn't have to ask me twice. At this point, there wasn't anything I wouldn't do for her. She need only ask.

I stood and walked toward her, kissing her hard. Her mouth was a flame, burning mine as I dropped my free hand—the one that wasn't still wrapped around my dick—to her clit. She whimpered with the first swirl of my fingertip, and it was my turn to moan into her mouth.

The desire to make her writhe, to make her scream, to make her come apart was too great to contain, and I knelt in front of her, prepared to worship her with my mouth, my hands, and my body. While Viktor continued to plunge in and out of her, slowly and sensually, I flicked my tongue out and swiped it along her clit. She wound her fingers into my hair, pulling, holding me to her while I continued licking and teasing her.

She pushed her leg onto my shoulder and the access was greater for both of us. I moaned against her, and she squirmed, but Vik held her hips as he increased his pace. She was passion and desire and perfection and as I knelt in front of her, I took out my cock and stroked it, using the bit of precum at the head to make it wet so my hand would glide along the skin as I squeezed and jerked.

After a few minutes, her body spasmed, tightened, went rigid and she cried out, curling her fingers in and out of my hair while Viktor continued pounding into her. I came watching her, then he came feeling her.

"Fuck." I whispered the word, though it wasn't like anyone would've heard me over the ocean and Viktor and Erin. I could safely say that if this was the way we were going to spend our days on the island, I could very much get into it.

When we were cleaned up and had checked on Silas, we sat on the beach with a bottle of wine, enjoying the day. I didn't know what they were thinking about, but I thought that if I had to be stuck on an uninhabited island with anyone, these people were probably the best choices.

The weather was mild, the sun warm. I sat wondering why no one had come for us... if we were so lost that we would never be found. But instead of speaking my thoughts, I kept them to myself. There was no point in making everyone else as anxious as I was.

Although an immense amount of guilt spun in my stomach. If not for me, if not for all this mess my proposed marriage to Posey had created, we wouldn't be in this situation. And there wasn't a fucking thing I could do to change any of it.

# CHAPTER 7

## ERIN

The island was beautiful. There was no doubt about that. But it was an island with no Starbucks, no Target, no carwash or gas station. No telephone service. No house or stove to cook on. Under other circumstances, one where I knew help was coming, this place might be a nice respite from life.

"Hey." Viktor's voice was soft as he laid his hand on my shoulder. "It's cooling off out here. We might need to start a fire."

He was right.

"I think we should not." Henryk shook his head and held up one finger. It was his way, and I found it endearing, but Viktor's forehead pinched. "If there are others on the island and they're dangerous, it could attract them."

Viktor laughed. "And maybe we can make a radio from coconuts, Gilligan."

I doubted Henryk would get the reference, but he narrowed his eyes as if he did, because the inference from Viktor's tone was most assuredly mocking.

"Don't speak to me as though I'm naïve or stupid," Henryk told Viktor. "We haven't explored the island or seen what lies on the other side. For all we know, there could be a resort over there." That would have been a dash of heaven. "There aren't many uninhabited islands in the world. What are the chances we would have found the only one unclaimed?"

That wasn't quite true, but Henryk was probably counting on the fact that we couldn't tell whether he was telling the truth or not. "We probably need to build a fire. A small one. For Silas, and I'm cold too. Plus, if there are animals, predators of the four-legged kind, the fire should keep them away." I was trying to keep the mood light. We'd all been through a lot. Tempers were short.

Standing, I brushed the sand off my jeans. "I'll do it myself." I wasn't being haughty or angry, I just wasn't going to listen to them argue. They both had points to make, but I didn't need to hear them. They could butt heads all night for all I cared. I was going to get firewood and build a fire.

Behind me, they argued for a couple more minutes as I walked down the beach, picking up driftwood then moved into the tall grasses. Finally, Henryk joined me. "You shouldn't be out here alone."

I shrugged. "You guys seemed to have something you needed to work out. I didn't want to be in the way." I was being nonchalant, as if mine wasn't the shortest temper of the bunch. I was trying to be a good sport about this. But the bickering had to stop. I wanted to say something, but I held it back in favor of keeping peace. My plan was to wait until they started again.

"You all right?" Henryk asked as he picked up a tree branch that had fallen.

"I could use an iced latte right now." It was true, but at the same time not. A latte wasn't going to fix much. What I needed was a satellite phone, a boat that didn't have its front half on the beach and its back half below sea level, a bed for Silas to rest and recuperate in, and a bit of bug repellent, since it was getting dark, and I couldn't see my feet in the tall grass.

"It's going to be okay," he promised, and although he spoke with plenty of conviction, I didn't find his words encouraging. Not one bit. I wasn't sure if I wanted his optimism or a bit of realism.

"Might be easier if you and Vik tried to get along." I shrugged. It shouldn't have been too much to ask. We were all in this together, would live or die together. I preferred to live. But that didn't mean we had to live like we were in an armed camp. There could be friendliness.

He nodded, and I got a good look at him with the sun setting behind him. He was a beautiful man, and it was no wonder he was a royal favorite. That wasn't just me saying it, either. Of all the royals in the world, Henryk was actually on some magazine's list of favorite royals and most beautiful people.

We gathered sticks and some bigger pieces of wood and carried them back to the beach. Henryk dug a hole with one of the pieces of wood, and then we arranged the wood and we looked at each other. Neither of us had a lighter or a book of matches.

Viktor moved away from Silas and came to where Henryk and I were both looking at the hole and our neat arrangement of sticks. He knelt in front of the hole and started some kind of voodoo magic with sticks until one was smoking and there was a small fire in our little pit.

"How did you do that?"

"Boy Scout Troop 147." Viktor smiled and held up his first two fingers. "I got the fire badge first out of my whole troop. My foster mother was convinced I was going to be an arsonist."

I didn't know a lot about how any of them grew up, but I knew he and Silas were tight because they shared history. That was likely why we were all so close. We had that moment from when we were kids, when there was only us on that playground, when nothing else mattered but the fact we were friends, and we didn't want that day to end.

It hadn't ended yet.

I glanced back at Silas, who was sleeping. And when I looked out at the water, there was a suitcase floating on the surface. I walked into the surf and stood in the gently rolling water. I didn't know whose bag it was, but it wasn't mine. That didn't mean there weren't things inside we could dry out and use.

Instead of waiting for it to float to me since I was excited about the prospect of something useful being inside, I walked further into the water and pulled it back to the beach with me. It was heavy and water-logged, but it was here. And no way in hell was I letting it float out to sea.

As I was walking back to the beach, dragging the bag along the sand, I looked further down the beach. In one of the trees about a hundred yards down the beach, the inflatable life raft was hanging in one of the palm trees.

If we could get it down, we could use it to sleep in, to protect us from slithering creatures that might have liked to take a big bite while we were still and sleeping. I'd been moderately worried about it since the sun started setting, and this was a perfect solution. Or it would have been perfect had the damned thing not been fifty feet in the air.

I looked at Henryk and Viktor, who were both staring at me, probably because I'd stopped walking and was standing with the suitcase at the edge of the beach. "You think we could get that thing down?" I pointed to the boat. It must have been some kind of wind that deposited it there. "We could sleep in it so the snakes..." I shuddered at the thought, didn't have to go on.

"I could climb up and give it a try." Henryk smiled, and I wondered if this was some odd testosterone competition because Viktor had managed to start a fire without flint, flame or matches, and so Henryk was going to prove how useful he was too.

He didn't wait for me to over-analyze the situation and took off toward the tree. Up close, it looked even taller than it did from down the beach. He stared for a minute, then rolled up his sleeves. Viktor stood beside me as Henryk started his way up the tree.

I folded my hands in front of my mouth and said a silent little prayer to whoever was listening and waited. He was about halfway to the top when something happened. He jerked one arm away and the other fell and then, as if he was moving in slow motion, he fell backward, landing hard enough the air whooshed out of him as I ran and dropped to my knees beside him.

He gasped and struggled, trying to draw breath and finally, after a few minutes, was breathing without gasping.

Viktor helped him sit up and I pulled Henryk against me. "Are you okay?"

He nodded. "I'm fine."

I wasn't so sure. His breaths were still short and shallow, but he was breathing, and that was enough for me. "I don't want you to try again." All I could think about were broken bones and the pain he would go through.

"I'm not itching to climb back up there." At least he smiled as he said it.

"You don't have to. I don't know what I was thinking." I shook my head. I was selfish. My fear of snakes had put Henryk in a position where he could have been seriously injured.

"I can make you a bed of palm leaves and we'll stay away from the grass."

"No. It's fine. I'll be fine. I was only scared of snakes." And a bed of palm leaves sounded like the kind of place a king cobra might have liked to snuggle up with me and eat his fill of crazy, stranded American.

Henryk slid his arm around me and pulled me in. "I'll stay awake while you sleep and make sure nothing happens and no snake comes near." He kissed the top of my head. "I'm not going to let anything happen to you."

When I looked up and into his eyes, I believed him. I believed he would do whatever he had to do to protect me. It didn't stop me from being scared that we were never going to make it home. That because I'd insisted he come with us to Ibiza, there was an entire nation that was going to be robbed of his ability to lead them into a bright future.

"You're trembling." He ran his hand down my back. I hadn't realized I needed comforting until now. He tilted my chin up and brought his mouth down to mine. When he pulled back, he smiled. "I'm not going to let anything happen to you."

I nodded because I believed him. I wanted to, anyway.

"And bringing you all to Lichtenstein was the best thing I've ever done. I don't regret one minute of this vacation." This time when he kissed me, it was deeper, with more feeling than before.

When we parted, I smiled at him. Being on the island with him and the others certainly wasn't the worst thing that could have happened to us, and it gave us a little more time together before the world came back and interfered.

We stood and walked back to where Silas was still passed out—maybe literally—on the beach. Viktor was sitting beside him but staring out into the surf. "How is he?"

"He's tough. Don't worry," Viktor said looking up at me and smiling.

But the bump on his head was turning a deep purple color and there was no denying he'd lost a lot of blood. There wasn't anything we could do but wait and pray. So I sat down beside him, took his hand in mine, and did the one thing I could do.

# CHAPTER 8

## VIKTOR

*Day 2*

Henryk and I took turns sleeping so that Erin wasn't afraid. The night was long and dark, with only a sliver of moon to light the sky. Here, though, there were stars. So many fucking stars, although they didn't help the darkness.

Erin slept peacefully, quietly, and more than once, I was tempted to check to make certain she was still breathing, but I didn't because that seemed creepy. And when she woke, she was even more beautiful than she'd been the day before. That was the thing with her. Every single time I looked at her, I could see something new about her that I hadn't noticed before. The sprinkling of freckles across the bridge of her nose that inched onto her cheeks and up to her forehead. The waves of gold in her dark hair. The flecks of blue and green and gold in her eyes. She was beautiful every minute of every day.

She sat up and brushed her hair back from her face. "Good morning."

Her smile was radiant. I'd never seen a woman so lovely in my life. And sometimes, it was easy to see a future for us—all of us.

Henryk put another armload of wood onto the fire even though we didn't need it for warmth now that the sun was back in its place. But if we were to be found, a plane would be able to see the fire. And we all had to assume that someone was out looking for us by now. At least, for him, and we would be found because of it. What happened after we were located was anyone's guess.

"Most boats are equipped with beacons for occasions such as this." He always chose phrasing that made him sound like a pompous prick. But then again, he usually was.

I wasn't quite at the point where I could refer to this as an *occasion* rather than the catastrophe it was. Silas was still on his back, in and out of consciousness. I was tired and worried. Erin was the one bright spot, and as beautiful as she was, she couldn't hide the fear in her eyes.

"Would a crash activate the beacon?" I had no knowledge about things like this. I wasn't a boat captain. Nor would I ever choose another boat as my chief mode of transportation for anything. I wasn't even so much as getting into a canoe. Hell, after this, there was a chance I wasn't going to take my chances with a body of water bigger than one of those kiddie pools the old ladies back home used to keep cool in their lawn chairs in the summer.

Henryk shrugged one shoulder but nodded his head. "I think so. I'm going to swim out and have a look."

I shook my head. "That's not a great idea. We can't all go." I motioned to Silas. "Someone has to stay here. And I don't want to leave Erin alone on the island."

"I could go with him." She raised her hand as if she were in class. "I can swim."

Henryk shook his head at just the moment I was about to say that wasn't ever going to happen. No way in fucking hell was I going to let her risk herself by swimming out to that boat. Not any more than I would let her try to climb up and retrieve that fucking rescue boat.

Henryk stared at her for a few long seconds before he spoke, as though I was going to have to step in anyway because he was thinking about letting her accompany him. "I can't be worried about you and still do what I must. I don't know where this box could be on this boat, and I need to explore."

"And I can't help?" Her brow pinched and her eyes narrowed. He'd offended her, and she wasn't about to let that pass. "I swim at home. I'm a strong fucking swimmer. And you shouldn't treat me like I'm fragile. *I* didn't fall out of a tree."

It was a low blow, and he narrowed his eyes for a second then a slow smile spread across his face. Then he laughed. "You're quite right. But let me go look for myself first. If I can't find it, we can swim out together." He shook his head. "I don't know exactly what the beacon looks like, so I don't know to tell you what to look for."

She didn't care. Her skin reddened as if she were angry, but she nodded anyway.

I didn't want to tell her that I agreed with him, that I didn't think I would be able to bear it if something happened to her. I also didn't want to tell her that I would rather die myself than to let her go down there. Mostly, I didn't share that because the word "let" wouldn't fly with her, and I wasn't in the mood for an argument. As much as I was trying to be a good sport, especially since this whole fucking excursion was my idea, it was my best friend, someone I considered a brother, who was still in and out of consciousness, and it was our contract we would lose if we weren't back in time. And it was a lot to know that every bit of it was my fault.

"What if it isn't there?" Erin asked, her eyebrows pinched together. "What if the guys who disabled the radio and took the jet skis and lifeboat off the ship took the beacon too, so we couldn't be found?"

There was an edge to her voice, a sharpness that made her sound almost frantic.

Henryk took her face in his hands and kissed her again. "It is part of the boat. Not something they would be able to easily remove." He sounded so certain, I almost believed him. "Don't worry, Erin. I'll be back in just a little while."

His confidence didn't waver. I admired that about him.

He stripped down to his boxers and walked into the water. He was waist-deep before he dove over a wave, and it took a couple long seconds for him to resurface. Then he swam. And swam. The boat was further out than it looked, and I was holding my breath waiting for him to get there.

I didn't always agree with him, but I considered him a friend, someone I would be very sorry to lose. So I was relieved that he resurfaced after a few minutes and swam back to the beach.

Erin walked into the water toward him. "Did you find it?"

He shook his head like a puppy, fast and chaotic, spraying the water in every direction so that it splattered on her, and she laughed, much lighter and more carefree than she'd been when he left to go to the boat. She hugged him and held on long enough that when she finally backed away, the front of her was soaked. It was a good look on her, especially when it happened with a smile.

"Don't worry," he finally said. "I'm going to rest for a few minutes and reset. And then I'll head back." But the look he shot me said he was more worried than he wanted to let on to her.

My stomach began to churn.

# CHAPTER 9

## HENRYK

*I* hated to see the worry darkening her eyes. This was a woman who couldn't hide any emotion she felt or thought she had. Everything showed on her face, in her eyes and in her expressions. I loved that about her. Hell, if I were honest, there wasn't much I didn't love about her. It was going to make marrying Posey difficult. I was never going to be able to stand up there and profess my undying devotion to any woman other than Erin. Not that I could ever imagine, anyway.

"Ray's going to find us." I said it in the most off-handed manner I could manage because I thought she needed some reassurance. And when she turned her beautiful smile toward me, I didn't care about anything else anymore.

"I know." But the sincerity wasn't there. She looked at me, trying, at least.

When she walked away to check on Silas, Viktor shot me a glare so deep his eyes were thin and probably crossed through their little slits. "You shouldn't give her false fucking hope, Gilligan."

I had no idea what he was talking about. I firmly believed that as we were arguing, Ray was out there, scouring the seas to find us. It was his job, and had I gone with my gut and let him onto the boat with us, no way would we have been in the situation.

But I had no idea why the fuck Viktor had called me *Gilligan,* or what the reference meant. Something told me, though, that it wasn't flattering. Not one fucking bit, and I didn't care for being mocked or taunted.

"Hey, Erin!" She looked up and smiled as though she had no idea what was happening right in front of her. I didn't know how she could be so oblivious, but I gave her the benefit of the doubt anyway. "Viktor just called me Gilligan, and I was wondering if you could clarify for me exactly who is Gilligan?" Not that it mattered in more than a sticks and stones childish kind of way.

She shot Viktor an eyeroll, and I wasn't sure if I'd annoyed her by not knowing who this Gilligan person was, or if he'd annoyed her for calling me that. But the scowl wasn't aimed at me.

She walked toward us, hips swaying, the view better than any sunset or sunrise or any other woman I'd ever seen. "*Gilligan,*" she said, still scowling at Viktor, "is a pop culture reference about a first mate who, with his captain, took a group of tourists on what was supposed to be a three-hour tour, but the weather kicked up and stranded them on an island. They were there for years." And then she sang a song about a fateful trip that started in a tropic port. It was quite a long song, but I sure as fuck didn't miss that the reference was unflattering. Still, the last thing we needed to do right now was get in each other's faces. "Funny."

Viktor held up his hands. "Truth is truth, *mate.*"

He was pissy. I understood it. He needed someone to blame, and it was easy to pass the buck when the responsibility for us being here rested solely on his fucking shoulders. Obviously, he hadn't done any kind of background check on the captain or crew of the boat. Hadn't checked the weather, watched the course we should've been on. Of course, none of us had done any of that, and now we were stranded. I could share some of the culpability for our predicament, but most of it belonged to him. He'd been neither diligent nor responsible.

"Of course, it is." If I sounded condescending, I couldn't help it.

He stepped forward. "You got something to say, rich boy? Something on your mind?" He poked me in the forehead.

But I could puff out my chest too. And I did. He needed to know exactly who the fuck he was dealing with. I was born to command an army. Born to rule a kingdom. I could take down one shockingly big American because I was made to do it. "As a matter of fact, when you booked our fancy accommodations on the Titanic's ugly cousin, did it occur to you that security might be a concern?"

"It wouldn't be if not for you. No one gives a fuck about three Americans traveling together. But anyone with a recent newspaper knows who you are and that you would be valuable in a ransom scenario." He crossed his arms and cocked his head with a *point made* smirk.

I couldn't deny it. "Perhaps, but I might have had Ray do what it is he's paid for and verified that we were dealing with a reputable company. Obviously, that concept escaped you."

"Fuck you, Fancy Pants."

"I'm already fucked, thanks to you." I stared hard. He didn't intimidate me. "You can call me *Gilligan* if you want, but I'm not the one who planned this trip, who got my friend injured, and who got us all stranded on this godforsaken fucking island."

And I didn't have to say any more. He knew it was the truth. "I didn't plan the storm."

"Didn't check the weather, either." I shrugged because we all knew I was right.

He shook his head as his nostrils flared, but then he turned and raked his hands through his hair. I didn't know if he was getting ready to turn around and clock me in the jaw or if he just needed a minute, so I waited.

"Fuck. I would kick your ass right now if you weren't right." He stared at me for a few long seconds then shook his head.

"You could try." Erin narrowed her eyes at me, so I softened the words with a smile and assumed a perfectly appropriate boxing stance, fists up and ready. "Hey, laugh if you want. I know I don't look like much in terms of muscle, but I'm wiry. Fast." I practiced some air boxing. The wind whipped me in the face, and I was battling it to perform my ever so intricate "boxing" moves, but I managed to make it look impressive enough.

He chuckled like he wasn't just about to pummel me. "Yeah, I can see that." And he held out his hand in that weird American handshake that was usually in the beer commercials. I managed to make it work, and then he pulled me in. "I'm sorry. I'm an asshole."

I nodded. "We can use your word." And then Erin tugged us each down to kiss our cheeks then she walked back to where Silas was awake now and watching. She was probably as tired of hearing the bickering as I was of being a part of it. We needed a truce, to knock it off.

He laughed. "Funny, the shit I keep waking up to." But he sounded better. Stronger, anyway, and Vik turned to look at him.

His smile moved across his face. His eyes crinkled at the corners. His best friend was awake. I glanced at the bruise on Silas's forehead. I didn't know what he'd hit or how hard he'd hit it, but it was a horrible deep purple.

More than the injury to his head, his leg was an issue. The bandages she'd put on there were soaked in red, and she stared too, but her smile never wavered even though her eyes went dark and there was an unusual tremble to her hands as she tended to the gash again.

Silas winced when she unwrapped the gauze, but he didn't make a sound more than sucking air between his teeth. I looked at the cut, didn't see anything I thought—although what did I know, really— meant the wound was infected, and she put another couple clean pads over it, then wrapped it in a round or two of gauze.

We didn't have any antiseptic or antibiotics to put on it, but I was still hopeful that we would be rescued with due haste. Someone had to be looking. Boats didn't just fall off the face of the earth. If Lichtenstein didn't send troops to find us, certainly the American government would send out people looking for its citizens.

Wouldn't they? Did anyone even know that Erin and the boys were missing?

I hoped so, anyway.

# CHAPTER 10

## ERIN

Certainly, there were worse places in the world that we could have been stranded. Places without glorious sunsets, without a white, sandy beach, without waves rolling in. It could've been like something from a bad scary movie. A place with skulls poking out of the sand and a boat that wasn't ours washed up on the sand with spiders and snakes and sea creatures crawling in and out of it. I could picture the other place in my head, and it wasn't pretty. It definitely wasn't somewhere I wanted to visit, by accident or not.

Although it would've been a much more pleasant trip if Henryk and Viktor called off their ridiculous bickering. Blaming one another. Bitching about who was in charge, and who would be the reason we survived. Not that I actually enjoyed not knowing how long we would be stranded here, but there were worse places. That was all I was saying. Thinking, anyway.

I hadn't stopped thinking about the fact that we hadn't seen the whole island. Maybe there was more than just our little part. Maybe there was a hotel on the other side. A resort. I saw it in a movie once. It could happen. That was what I told myself as I looked over at Silas. Obviously, he couldn't go, but if we found something useful on the other side—a resort would certainly be helpful. Hell, at this point a canoe would've made me happy.

"Maybe we should check out the other side of the island." I looked at Silas. "I could stay with you, and they could go."

"You want to put Curly and Moe in charge of our big escape?" He smiled, and it was adorable. More so because I'd seen the cut, doctored and dressed it. And there was no way he wasn't in pain.

Henryk grumbled, and Viktor shook his head but he was smiling. "Hey, Larry. Unless you're ready to go for the big swim, we're the best shot you have to get out of here in one piece." He must have been relieved to see his best friend awake and teasing them. It accounted for his smile, anyway.

I looked at Silas because I hadn't yet answered his question. "I don't want to have to choose one of them to go with me." I smiled because that was one of those truths I didn't really realize was true until I said it.

"I feel you." And then he wagged his eyebrows and winced for the effort. I wasn't sure which part of him hurt worst, but our bottled water supply was dwindling as was our pain relief packets that were part of the first aid kit.

"Are you all right?" I hated to see anyone in pain, ever more when it was someone I cared about. I laid my hand on his arm as he closed his eyes and blew out a breath.

"Yeah. There are just a couple things I don't think I'm quite ready for." He laid back against the clothes from the suitcase that I'd wadded and put under his head. "I need a minute."

I nodded at him while my stomach rolled with worry. I should've gone to medical school. Should've paid attention in health class. If something happened to him—and by now I was thinking infection or worse—I would never survive it.

I glanced over my shoulder at Viktor and Henryk. "Find us help." Henryk nodded and Viktor gave a solemn smile.

"Should we have a signal in case there's something dangerous? On either side?"

"We could yell something like, I don't know, *HELP*, maybe!" I demonstrated at scary movie girl screech and volume.

Henryk laughed and Viktor nodded. "*Help* it is, then."

I stood for a kiss from Viktor that made my heart race and another from Henryk that made my belly twist. These were all men who knew how to use their mouths in the best ways, and I was so lucky to benefit from it.

When I sat and turned back to Silas, his eyes were closed, and I laid beside him, put my head on his chest, breathed a little easier when he curled his arm around me. "We're going to be okay, Erin."

"You have a crystal ball I don't know about?" I tried to keep it light because my eyes were watering.

"No, but I have faith. And we just found one another again." I turned my chin up and stared at him. His eyes were still closed, but his smile was real, and it was exactly what I needed. "No way would fate or any higher power would let us lose each other now."

I nodded. "I hope so."

He moved enough to kiss the top of my head then tightened his arm around me. "You know, Erin, if I died here, I wouldn't go unhappy."

"That's very sweet." I chuckled. "I think." But I continued smiling at him because I felt the same way. In all my life, I'd never known the kind of happiness I've had since I got the call from Henryk and arrived at Lichtenstein and saw them all again.

The others hadn't been gone long, but I wanted them to come back. "Erin? Are you all right?"

I shook my head. Certainly, I wasn't all right. I wasn't home with a blanket on my legs watching some show on Netflix that I'd already seen ten or so times. And I was worried. "I just can't stop thinking that while we don't know if there's a resort on the other side of the island, we also don't know if there is a family of hillbillies who would happily feed us to their pigs, or a serial killer in hiding, or if the kidnappers are on the other side of the island watching us."

He laughed. "I was hoping we were on some million-dollar reality show."

I laughed too. And it felt good to laugh, to have a moment of relief from the heaviness. I was holding it together at this point, but barely, and it wouldn't take much for me to lose my shit and freak out on any one or LL of them.

"Can you imagine if there is a resort over there?"

I nodded. "With a doctor and a spa."

"A five-star chef." We both sighed, then he glanced at me at the same moment I glanced at him, and we laughed. "I could go for some braised beef right now."

At the mention of food, I moved away and picked up a can and turned it so I could read the label. "You mean, you aren't looking forward to our dinner of pork and beans and the last banana?" I wanted to be fun and funny, to make this whole thing an adventure, and I was trying, but it fell short.

"Pork and beans are a personal favorite."

I leaned in and pressed a kiss to his mouth, waited for him to kiss me back then fell back onto the sand beside him as he used his tongue to explore mine.

When we parted, he brushed his fingers across my forehead, pushing my hair from my face. "Being beside you makes me want—"

"Want?" A warm purr started in my belly and worked its way through my body. I knew a thing or two or ten about wanting. And thanks to them, about getting. I also knew a thing or two about losing, and I wasn't in a place where I wanted that to happen now. Or even when we returned to Lichtenstein. So maybe being here on this island wasn't the worst thing. Not for me, anyway.

But I wasn't the one who was injured and probably in pain.

He nodded and lowered his head again. "I want you. I want us. I want… everything."

So did I. He leaned his forehead against mine then moved a bit more carefully to one side, so I wasn't touching the ugly purple bump on his head. "Me, too."

"Isn't it weird that there's no one here and this island is empty?" He looked around as though he might have expected to see someone other than us on this part of the beach.

He had a point, though. In this day and age, property was claimed for one country or another, bought, paid attention to. I nodded. "Maybe it's one of those private islands where the owner has it just so he can say he owns an island in the… ocean." I had no idea where we actually were. Maybe if we hadn't been kidnapped, it would've been easy to figure out. I couldn't see another land formation anywhere. All I could see was miles and miles of water. So much water.

"We could go full Brooke Shields and the blond kid. Remember that movie? Where they were stuck on an island and they built a hut. And the professor and Maryanne were there with their coconut radio?" He had his stories mixed up and I suspected it was on purpose.

I laughed. "You want to build a hut?"

"And you can weave a hammock from… I have no idea." But he was awake and smiling, and I liked to think he was having fun. That was enough for me. For now, anyway.

The later in the day it became, the more I worried about Henryk and Viktor. I hadn't heard a shouted or screechy *help*, but that didn't mean they hadn't found an island creature who was angry we were infiltrating its turf, or maybe some old mean guy who'd been alone on the island for fifty years and didn't like us intruding.

The thoughts in my head were scattered. And the fear was real and intense and increasing ever so steadily.

Silas closed his eyes and laid back under the canopy of one of Viktor's shirts from a second suitcase that washed ashore this afternoon. It wasn't a long moment before he fell back to sleep and every moment he slept, worried me more.

I stayed beside him even as the sun moved across the afternoon sky. Even as the day started changing to evening, and they still hadn't returned. Even as the urge to go find them was strong and I wanted to go looking. But I stayed because we couldn't all be in charge, and there was enough bickering between all of them. Besides, I'd agreed—hell, I'd volunteered—to stay with Silas.

Silas woke once more and looked down the beach. "They aren't back yet?"

I shook my head and looked off in the direction from which they'd left. There was no sign they were coming back from that direction, but it made the most sense in my mind for whatever reason. But the beach stayed quiet. The sun continued to move across the sky. Silas tried—oh, how he tried—to lighten the mood.

"Knock, knock."

I sighed because I wasn't in the mood for a joke session. "Not now, okay, Silas?"

"Knock, knock." Persistence was one of his more prevalent traits.

"Who's there?" And there wasn't much point in denying him. Chances were, unless I walked away, he was telling this joke.

"Weirdo." His grin was still quite mesmerizing, and I stared for a few seconds before I shook my head.

"Weirdo, who?"

"Weirdo you think they are?" He chuckled and pulled me down so I was lying beside him then wrapped me in a hug. I felt safe and protected, and I wanted to sink into the feeling. More so when he kissed my forehead and whispered, "Don't worry. Viktor could wrestle a grizzly bear and come out on top."

I didn't doubt it, but that also didn't make me worry any less. I wanted them to come back, and I wanted them to do it right now.

# CHAPTER 11

## VIKTOR

The island wasn't in fact a resort. It was an overgrown piece of land with very few redeeming qualities. There was a white sandy beach, which was nice. There were crystal clear waters at the edge of the beach. There were fish that we could catch without much trouble, so we wouldn't starve. So there was that. But this was a lot more like Gilligan's Island than I'd thought at first glance. And it was probably below the belt to call Henryk Gilligan, especially since this whole thing was my fault, but in the moment, it slipped out.

And I needed to apologize. "Look, Henryk, what I said earlier…" He turned his head to look at me, and he could've just as easily punched me as nodded at me. But he didn't lift his hand. He didn't get angry. It spoke to his character. No matter what kind of pain in my ass he was, he was also a good man. And that meant something to me. "I was being a dick."

"Yeah." He chuckled. "I get it. It's a tough situation we're in. Tempers flare." He shrugged as though he waere over it. "I'm not holding anything against anyone on this trip. I know why you did this, why you planned it, and I'm grateful."

"You worried about the wedding?" It was a reasonable concern. He was betrothed, not engaged. Engagement was a choice. Betrothal was an obligation. I would have my tightie whities in a twist too, maybe be a little more unreasonable than he is.

"Not the wedding. The marriage and the lifetime of logistics that will go along with it." He spoke solemnly and quietly, as if he thought he might have been followed. Again. It couldn't be easy to be him.

That meant this—being on the island—was his last chance to be with Erin, to be part of this thing we had going on. "That sucks."

He nodded.

We'd been walking for a while. If I had to guess, I would have said that the island was probably a good ten miles around. Maybe ten across, too. I ran that distance in the morning, and it didn't take an entire afternoon, but we weren't on a leisurely run. We were looking for something—anything—on the island that might help us or save us.

We hadn't found much. There were tall grasses, some plants and berries that were edible going by the dead red rule –they were black berries and blue ones. Wild, of course.

When I was about to suggest we head back, go the rest of the way tomorrow, Henryk grabbed my arm and pointed. "Hey, look."

The cabin was small, but a cabin. Shelter that meant someone else had been here. Possibly still here. "What do you think?" Henryk asked as we crouched, moving closer for a better look.

I smiled. "Looks like a safe haven to me." But when I stood to move in, he pulled me back down.

"It could be that this island is used for drug runners." He nodded. "A stopover or a meeting place." It wasn't like we weren't going to go in, but he was saying we needed to be careful.

I got it. "Could be just the summer place of a rich guy who lives in one of those cold-ass countries and likes his tropical seasons." I wasn't your typical bright side of life kind of guy, but I also didn't want to think this island was a cartel hideaway. "I don't know exactly where we are, but I don't think we're close enough to anything for this cabin to be convenient for a drug runner."

We remained half crouched as we moved closer. The place wasn't exactly a shack. It was big and had a combination lock on the door. It also had windows, and one at the back of the place was open. There was a porch along the back with a weathered rocking chair under an awning that was retractable but had been left open.

It was enough to make me wonder if someone else was currently on the island.

Henryk stepped onto the porch and tried the door, turned to look at me when it opened. He poked his head in, hand still on the doorknob in case he needed to pull it shut in a hurry. "Hello?" He waited a second then tried again. "Hello?" He looked back at me. "I don't hear anything inside."

I was standing off to the side of the porch. "So what do you want to do? Should we go in?"

He nodded. "I think so."

So far today, we'd seen a small mountain ending as a cliff that would've been ideal for cliff diving had there not been about a thousand rocks in the cove it overlooked. We saw some plants. Some birds that were exotic and thin, probably not much in the way of food for us. And I wasn't itching to try to trap one because the beaks on those things, whatever they were, were sharp and pointed. Not something I wanted to battle in hand-to-hand combat. We'd seen some clouds that had disappeared as quickly as we'd seen them and hadn't produced much more than a drizzle.

But the only thing we'd seen that had given me any hope whatsoever, was this cabin. Someone knew about this island. Someone who had been here in the recent past. And that meant we weren't off the grid or the map. Not entirely.

Henryk pushed the door until it swung all the way around on its hinges and touched the wall inside the cabin. He called out one last time before crossing the threshold. When no one jumped out to attack us, I followed him in.

"It doesn't look like anyone's been here for some time." Henryk dragged his finger through a layer of dust on the small kitchen table.

"Maybe they're just not big on housekeeping. Not everyone has a staff of maids and butlers at their disposal." I don't know why I felt the need to tease him about his money at every opportunity, except for the fact that I'd spent the majority of my life without any.

Henryk didn't ask to be born into a life of luxury, and it wasn't without its own unique set of problems. But whoever said money can't buy happiness never grew up poor.

"Let's just hope they left behind something we can use." Henryk chose to ignore the cheap shot and started rummaging through the few cupboards on the wall above the counter.

"I'll check out the bathroom and then head into the bedroom. Maybe there's a first aid kit that wasn't waterlogged. Silas needs a hell of a lot more than what you and Erin pulled from the wreckage."

Henryk closed the first empty cabinet and glanced over his shoulder. "Any medicine you're lucky enough to find is likely expired. We don't want to risk Silas' condition by doing more harm than good."

"Old Tylenol is better than no Tylenol." I left the prince in the kitchen and went about my own search for supplies in the abandoned cabin.

Unfortunately, the previous occupants didn't leave much behind. There wasn't as much as a sliver of soap in the bathroom and the bedroom wasn't much better. A couple of tattered books, raggedy blankets and something that might have passed for a pillow a decade earlier. I could only hope that Henryk found something useful in the kitchen.

"I got nothing." If the bedroom had a door, I would have slammed it behind me. The only thing left to take my frustrations out on was the prince and I'd used him as a punching bag one too many times on this vacation from hell as it was.

"I'm afraid I didn't fare much better." Henryk gestured toward his small haul of supplies spread out on the table.

A lantern with a few drops of kerosene left in the filler cap, a couple cans of baked beans and a half empty box of matches.

"Great, more beans." I grabbed a can from the table and checked the expiration date. "Why is it always beans? I mean, how often do people actually eat them in the course of a week anyway? Never mind, you've probably never eaten a can of baked beans in your life."

"Actually, this may come as a shock to you, but when I was a young boy living in Washington D.C. I was quite the finicky eater. Our cook introduced me to an American favorite—beans and weenies." Henryk folded his arms across his chest, closing himself off as if my questioning baked beans had somehow offended him. "I ate it several times a week."

"Bullshit," I scoffed and barked out a laugh of disbelief. "There is no way your royal highness, with a personal chef at his beck and call, ate canned beans with little chunks of hot dogs stirred into it."

"I assure you, I did. Much to my mother's disgust and disappointment." Henryk smiled at the childhood memory, and it was clear what Erin still saw in him… what we all saw in him on the playground all those years ago.

"You should add it to the menu for the wedding reception," I joked and set the expired can of beans on the table. They were out of date, but not so old we needed to worry about botulism or something.

Henryk doubled over with full-bodied laughter, his right arm wrapped around his middle and his left palm braced against his knee. "That's a marvelous idea. I'll be sure to mention it to Posey and the wedding coordinator when we get back to Lichtenstein."

"*If we get back*, you mean," I muttered under my breath. The odds of us making it off this island grew slimmer by the minute. When Henryk asked what I'd said, I waved him off and scooped up the supplies he found. "Let's just get these back to the beach."

"I was thinking." Henryk paused and cleared his throat. "That rather than bringing the supplies to Erin and Silas, we should bring them here, to the cabin, instead."

"I'm not sure that's a good idea. At least not yet." I glanced around the cabin again, observing its neglected condition. "Just because this place looks abandoned doesn't mean that it is. We should wait, stake it out, make sure no one shows up. Better safe than sorry, you know?"

That was an iconic piece of advice coming from me, considering I was the reason we were stranded on an island to begin with. Henryk, to his credit, was gracious enough not to rub it in my face. I doubted if I would have done the same if the shoe were on the other foot. Not that that would ever happen. The prince erred on the side of caution, and I wouldn't be caught dead in his overpriced, fancy-ass shoes.

"I'm not sure waiting a couple of hours will make a difference." He motioned toward the door and the patch of jungle outside. "We haven't seen signs of another soul since we've been here, but if it makes you feel better, we can wait."

"If you want to put Erin and Silas's safety at risk, by all means, run down to the beach like the hero you think you are, Fancy Pants."

"I don't pretend to be anything. I am and have been from the first moment you arrived in my country, completely open about who and what I am. Can you say the same? I am starting to suspect the answer is no." Henryk's expression darkened as he stalked toward the door. "And for the record, my fancy pants aren't what landed us in the mess. It was your incredibly thick head."

The prince stormed off, slamming the weather-worn door hard enough to rattle one hinge loose from the jamb. He was pissed. Not only that, but he was right.

And I was going to have to eat a heaping helping of humble pie. All I had to do was swallow my pride first.

# CHAPTER 12

## HENRYK

My temper had gotten the best of me, something that seemed to be happening with more frequency as of late. As a devoted prince and son, I'd learned to school my features and keep a tight rein on my emotions, but the more time I spent around my childhood friends, the less ability I had to apply those lessons. Viktor was especially good at pushing my buttons and cracking my control.

Almost as good as Erin.

The only difference was, I wanted her to. Somewhere along the line, I'd fallen hard for the buxom beauty with her bubbly personality and adventurous spirit. But the truth of it was, Erin stole my heart on the playground all those years ago and never gave it back. Not even when I asked her for a very official divorce to a very unofficial and unorthodox wedding.

I was supposed to sow my wild oats on this trip, prepare myself for a life devoted to crown and country. But now? It was hard to see a future without Erin in it. I was torn between the woman I loved and the country I was devoted to. Of course, there was a way that I could have it all—the crown, the throne, a life with Erin—but I could never ask that of her. Nor would she agree. As much as I wanted Erin in my bed every night, it wasn't fair if she couldn't stand by my side every day.

And even if my obligations to the throne and to Posey were removed from the equation, I still wasn't certain that was the life she wanted.

Erin was a passionate woman in and out of the bedroom. She was drawn to Silas and Viktor, and both men brought something out of her, filling a need that she seemed unaware of until our reunion. She wouldn't choose me. Not when she could have Viktor and Silas as a package deal. They knew how to share, to be in a relationship with more than one partner, whereas I still had a lot to learn.

Our problem wasn't in the bedroom but out of it, and one I wasn't sure we could fix. As much as I wanted Erin and the life she had to offer, it felt more out of reach than ever before.

But none of that mattered, at least for the time being. We were stranded on a deserted island with little to no food, fresh water, or medical supplies to tend to Silas's injuries. Finding a way off the island was the number one priority. Everything else could wait.

After all, there was no future with or without Erin if we didn't survive.

"Hey, Fancy… er, Henryk, wait up a second." Viktor gripped the railing, putting more faith in the rotten wood than I would have, and swung himself off the porch. "I'm sorry, man. I don't know why I lash out. I don't mean to."

"It's a defense mechanism. Rather than admit your faults or mistakes, you deflect and redirect your frustrations at the easiest target. Right now, you seem to be under the impression that that is me." I straightened my spine, rising to my full height and broadening my chest and shoulders. "I'm trying my best for Erin's sake not to be goaded into an argument, but I am no one's whipping boy."

"Right, you're a prince. You have one of your own. I don't need you to psychoanalyze me, *your highness*." Viktor raked his hand through his hair and belted out a colorful string of profanity. "Sorry, I'm doing it again. You're right. I'm an asshole."

The defeated look in his eyes and tone in his voice gave me pause.

"Look, we're in a horrible situation. Tempers are high and morale is low." I blew out a breath and extended my hand. "Let's just put this behind us and start over."

"I'm not sure how many times we can start over." Viktor barked out an awkward laugh and clasped my hand in his. "But I appreciate it, and since we're starting over, *again*, I need to come clean about something."

"I'm listening." I let go of his hand and sat on a tree stump at the edge of the trail that led back down to the beach.

There wasn't much Viktor could say that I didn't know or at the very least suspect, but it was clear he needed to get it off his chest. It cost me nothing but time to hear him out. And at the moment, time was something I had plenty of.

"This vacation from hell is my fault. It was my idea to set sail rather than fly back. I wanted to buy us all a little more time together, and thought we'd be safe out at sea, far away from the paparazzi and your brother's drones." Viktor rolled a section of axe hewn log out of the brush, set it beside mine and sat down. "We've been riding on your dime this whole time. Which, don't get me wrong, all expenses paid is great, but I wanted this to be from me. Except I couldn't even do that. I dropped your name to score a good price. It never occurred to me that I would be putting a target on your back."

"Why would you? It's not something you're used to thinking about. It's not as if someone would have a reason to abduct you." I shook my head, scoffing at my own choice of words. "Sorry, that came out wrong. I hope my poor choice of words didn't offend you."

"No harm, no foul. I get what you mean." Viktor clasped a hand on my shoulder and gave a reassuring squeeze. "You're right. Nobody ever wanted to kidnap me, and I'm pretty sure if they did, they would have brought my stubborn ass right back."

"I don't blame you, not really. I suppose I did at first, but that was just my emotions getting the better of me." I paused and smiled at him. It was my turn to be honest about the so-called blame and responsibility for how we ended up on this island. "And misdirecting them."

"I'm glad you pointed that out. I'd hate to call you a hypocrite after we just called a truce." Viktor laughed and landed a soft bump on my bicep with his fist.

"If the blame lies at anyone's feet, it's mine. I should have known better than to send Ray ahead and go on a trip without him at my side." I propped my elbows on my knees and rested my head in my hands, bracing myself for the swell of darkness that always followed the memories I was about to share. "Modern day pirates and paparazzi aren't the only reason we're so paranoid about my security. Neither is my brother. When I was a young boy, not long after I met the three of you, I was taken."

"Taken?" Vitkor sucked in a breath between his teeth and adjusted his position on the log, turning to face me. "As in kidnapped?"

I nodded and swallowed the lump in my throat. "We never spoke about it. Abduction wasn't appropriate conversation during a seven-course meal, and therapy was out of the question. God forbid the press got wind that the heir to the throne was in therapy, or tabloid bribes reached a level worthy of a psychologist breaking doctor-patient privilege."

"For fuck's sake, man." Viktor seemed to be at a loss for words. "That's really…"

Not that I blamed him. What was he supposed to say? Nothing he said would or could change the past or the way my family handled it. The rift was there, and while I lived to fulfill my obligation to them and Lichtenstein, things were never the same between us.

Erin, Silas and Viktor had done more to heal my wounds and erase the scars no one else could see. Their actions saved me in a way no words ever could. The way they made me feel when I allowed myself to be free of my title's shackles, filling a void no one else ever could, was the only therapy I needed.

"Yeah, don't let the regal robes and jeweled crowns fool you." For a moment, I dropped the prim and proper speech drilled into me since boyhood, sounding more like Silas and Viktor. "My family is just as fucked up as everyone else's. There were only two of them, but they were coordinated, methodical and ruthless. By the fourth day, I learned how much pain a person can inflict on another and still provide proof of life. But it could have been worse. The men who abducted me were brutal bastards, but they weren't child predators. They were in it for the money, and my parents paid the ransom. Interpol tracked the money and moved in for an arrest. The kidnappers opened fire, choosing to go out in a hail of bullets rather than dying in a prison cell like they deserved."

Viktor's gaze raked over me, searching for any remaining signs of the physical trauma I endured at the hands of my captors.

"You won't find any." I uttered a soft, but bitter laugh.

"Find any what?" He had the decency to look sheepish for staring.

Not that I cared. I was the one who chose to share this piece of my past with him and lay myself bare, exposing myself in a way I hadn't when the four of us had been caught in the throes of passion and intimacy.

"Scars." I waved a hand in front of me, gesturing from head to toe. "My mother enlisted the best plastic surgeons money could buy. Skin grafts, laser surgery, whatever it took and whatever it cost to ensure I remained the perfect prince. At least on the outside."

"What the fuck is it with family?" Viktor scratched the stubble along his jaw that would fill out into a short beard within a day or two. "The people who are supposed to love you are the ones that hurt you the most."

I knew about his upbringing, or the lack thereof. He'd fallen through the cracks of a system underfunded, understaffed and over-loaded with cases. Logistical red tape often made it easier for adoption of children abroad than those at home, leaving far too many bouncing from one foster home to another. Viktor had been one of those children. The one constant and saving grace in his life was his friendship with Silas. He was the closest thing to family Viktor ever had.

It surprised me how much I wanted to change that and just how much I wanted Erin, Silas, Viktor and me to act on the bond we shared. To be together, to have a future together.

The sun fell behind the palm trees, transitioning the bright blue sky to soft shades of pink and purple. A hush fell over the rainforest as the animals foraging during the day settled in to sleep and for protection against the dangerous predators who prowled the night.

"Well, what do you think? Should we head back or buckle down for the night?" Viktor asked, offering me an opportunity to take the lead and make the decisions.

It was an olive branch, and one I was relieved to accept.

"It's getting dark and will be even darker further in the jungle along the trail. We should hunker down for the night. Stumbling upon a poisonous spider, venomous snake, or worse, a jungle cat, is a risk we can't afford to take."

Not with one of us already injured.

"Sounds like a plan to me. Plus, it'll give us a few more hours to keep an eye on the place. See if anyone comes back." Viktor got to his feet, rolled his makeshift log stool into the bushes, taking shelter under the broad canopy of philodendron leaves. "I just have one question. Which do you think is more deadly? A panther or Erin when we get back down to the beach in the morning?"

I joined in his laughter and pushed my chunk of fallen tree under the leaves beside him.

The answer to his question was obvious—Erin.

# CHAPTER 13

## ERIN

*Day 3*

"Where the hell have the two of you been?" I stormed toward them, as much as the beach would allow a person to storm, kicking up grains of sand as I went. "Silas and I have been worried sick. How could you do that to him, knowing the condition he's in?"

"It's cool, guys. I wasn't that worried." Silas withered like a blossom under the rays of the noonday sun in the middle of a summer drought when I rounded on him, leveling him with my deadliest glare.

"We have been out of our minds with worry." In truth, I had been the one who was worried out of her mind. Silas tried and failed to soothe my frayed nerves. I thought seeing them safe and sound would calm me down, but it only fired me up even more. "We hardly slept at all, and you know how important it is for Silas to rest so he can recover."

"I told you, man." Viktor gave Henryk a light jab in the ribs with his elbow. "She's way more dangerous than any jungle cat."

"You think this is funny? That our being stranded here and Silas's leg being all messed up is just a big joke?" The stress of the situation had gotten to me, and I felt ready to crack under the pressure. It wasn't fair to lash out the way I did, but I couldn't help myself. I'd uncorked my emotions, and they all came pouring out.

"Of course, not." Henryk dropped the small bundle of supplies cradled against his chest and caught my wrist before I could land a second smack to his muscled shoulder. "We never meant to cause you a moment of concern, my darling, but neither of us felt we could risk the jungle at night."

He pulled my hand to his mouth, kissing my palm, my wrist, the inside of my elbow and worked his way to the crook of my neck. My body betrayed my mind, shifting the fire within me from my temper to fan the flames of passion building between my legs. My body molded to his, every hard plane pressed against my soft curves. He was impossible to resist, and now that he was back, safe in my arms, I didn't want to.

Viktor moved up behind me, anchoring his arm around Henryk's waist so that I was wedged firmly between them, and I meant firm. I tilted my head back, resting it against Viktor's chest and parted my lips in an invitation for him to kiss me. He accepted, covering my mouth with his and slipping his tongue inside.

I deepened the kiss, moaning into his mouth when Henryk dipped his head and nipped at my nipple, working the sensitive flesh between his teeth and the thin fabric of my shirt.

"Silas," I gasped, breaking from Viktor's kiss long enough to catch my breath. "We shouldn't. Not without him."

I turned, as much as I could, sandwiched between Henryk and Viktor, and looked at him. His hand was buried beneath the waistline of his shorts. When our gazes locked and he knew he had my attention, he used his other hand to undo the button and zipper and exposed the full length of his magnificent cock. He tightened his grip on the shaft, squeezing on the upward stroke until the tip glistened with precum.

That was all the permission I needed. Silas liked to watch, and if he was going to sit this one out, the least I could do was give him one hell of a show.

I stepped out from between Viktor and Henryk, shimmied out of my clothes, and got down on all fours while keeping my focus on Silas. This was as much for him as it was for the rest of us. We all needed a release, both mental and physical.

Henryk stripped out of his clothes, exposing his glorious, muscled physique and knelt in front of me, cock in hand. He slid his hand back and forth in long, slow strokes until I took him in my mouth, flicking my tongue along the sensitive spot on the underside of the tip.

Viktor wasted no time shedding his clothes and joining us on the sand. His body was chiseled planes and hardest where it mattered most. He knelt behind me, gripped my ass and buried himself inside me.

My moans of pleasure were muffled with my lips wrapped around the girth of Henryk's cock. I loved the way these men completed me, filled me in a way I never thought possible and yet somehow, I wanted more, needed more of them. Whoever said there was such a thing as too much of a good thing had never met Viktor, Silas or Henryk.

I ground my hips against Viktor, all but begging him to fuck me, while I bobbed my head up and down, licking and sucking the length of Henryk's cock.

"Fuck me, Erin. Your pussy feels so good." Viktor's hands slid down around my hips, holding me still. His fingers pressed into my flesh as he tightened his grip and picked up the pace, thrusting harder, faster.

Henryk raked his hands through my hair, twisting it around his fingers and gave a gentle tug, subtly asking for control. I was more than happy to oblige. He slid in and out of my mouth, matching Viktor's pace as he pumped himself in and out of my pussy. They were pleasuring themselves, pleasuring me, and we fed off each other's desires. The pressure of my orgasm built and built until it felt like I was going to explode, and I wasn't the only one.

Silas was right there with me. We'd positioned ourselves in the sand within arm's reach if he wanted to touch any one of us, and in direct line of sight with me. I wanted to watch him watching me as he ran his hand up and down the length of his cock, pleasuring himself.

We were close, so close, and when he reached beneath me, slipping his hand between my legs and fingering my clit, I came undone. My orgasm hit hard and fast, milking Viktor's cock as he pumped harder and faster before he pulled out and came on my back. Henryk tugged my hair, pulling my attention from Silas as his cock pulsed in my mouth and his salty cum spilled down my throat.

We collapsed on the sand beside Silas, careful to avoid his injured leg, in a tangle of arms and legs. Our flushed bodies pressed against each other as we basked in the euphoria and comforted one another until the grit of sand on my body forced me into the surf to clean off.

After a quick rinse in the ocean, I threw on my clothes and joined Henryk and Victor alongside Silas as they regaled him with their adventure into the jungle. They'd found a small cabin nestled in the palms that appeared to be abandoned. There was some debate about whether or not we should break camp on the beach and take shelter there.

"What about getting rescued? I don't know about you guys, but I wasn't *really* looking to make this island vacation permanent. If we move off the beach, there won't be anyone here watching for passing ships or planes." Silas's skin paled and beaded with sweat.

It seemed our little sexual escapade had been too much for him. I should have known better. His leg was bad, and he still showed signs of a concussion. Guilt over possibly worsening his condition washed away the small sting his words had unintentionally caused.

I knew we couldn't stay on the island forever. And truth be told, without at least a couple modern conveniences like indoor plumbing, I didn't want to. But our being together, away from prying eyes and the pressures and responsibilities of the real world, was wonderful and difficult to give up despite the fact that we all had lives of our own waiting for us. Not to mention the fact that Silas was in stable condition, but he still needed medical care.

Rescue meant reality, and I wasn't sure that I was ready for it. The cabin seemed like a wonderful way to delay the inevitable, but if the grimace and wince were any indication, Silas was in no condition for a trek through the rainforest.

"Silas is right." I caught Henryk and Viktor's gazes as they turned their attention toward me. "Maybe not for the reasons he thinks, but we should stay on the beach. He's not going to be able to hike up to some cabin on his own and he doesn't look up to being carried there either. At least not tonight."

"Perhaps you're right." Henryk got to his feet and brushed the sand from his clothes. "It will be getting dark soon. I'll gather some more driftwood for the fire."

"Hold up, your highness." Viktor hopped up, his feet sinking in the hot sand as he plodded after Henryk. "I'll give you a hand."

"Do you feel up to helping me prepare dinner?" I gave Silas a little wink and grabbed a couple of the cans the guys had brought down from the cabin.

"What's on the menu, chef?" Silas's smile brightened his face and added some much-needed color to his cheeks.

"Let's see what we've got to work with. Pork and beans." I shook an aluminum can that was missing its label. "And peaches or maybe it's pears."

"Sounds delicious. A meal fit for a king." Silas chuckled. "Or at least for a prince stranded on a deserted island."

Viktor and Henryk returned, arms laden with small logs, branches and dried out sea grass for kindling, and started fire. We sat together, basking in the warmth of the flames and shared our small feast, passing the cans of beans and what turned out to be pears drenched in heavy syrup. Thank goodness the cans had snap off lids.

The rainforest fell quiet as the birds and smaller animals settled down for the night for sleep and refuge from the jungle cats prowling the forest. Henryk propped himself up against the old, half rotten tree trunk beside Silas and took the first watch while the rest of us caught a few hours of sleep.

The sun crested the horizon, bringing warm rays and a new day. Too bad it was filled with more of the same. No boats, no planes, no signs of rescue. Our supplies were running low, and the boys continued to discuss whether the four walls and a roof up at the cabin were better than staying exposed, hoping for a rescue out on the beach.

But it didn't matter where we slept unless we had food.

"I'm going back to the boat." I pushed myself up on my feet, brushed myself off and marched toward the water.

"Guys." Silas tried to get Viktor and Henryk's attention behind me, giving a loud whistle when they talked over his first attempt. "Erin's going off on an adventure. Thought you might want to know."

The two of them joined me at the surf, the water lapping at our feet before being pulled back out to sea to form another wave.

"Whoa, hold up sweetheart." Viktor slipped his hand in mine and tugged me back toward our makeshift camp. "Why don't you let Henryk or me go? You can keep taking care of Silas."

"Why? Because taking care of a wounded man is a woman's work?" I rounded on him, jamming my hands down on my hips in an aggressive stance.

"Uh…no…I…" Viktor stammered.

"What our friend is trying to say, my darling, is you're running on fumes, weary, and haven't had enough calories for such an exerting swim." Henryk came to Viktor's rescue.

Not that he should have needed saving in the first place, especially from me.

Henryk was right. I was exhausted and starving. Neither were good reasons for taking my frustrations out on Viktor, but they were good enough reasons for me to swim back out to the shipwreck.

"It's sweet how much you all worry about me, and I appreciate it. Really, I do. But we all know I'm a stronger swimmer than either of you." I tossed my shirt and shorts on the beach and headed back to the surf.

Clouds moved in, blocking the sun and blue sky from view. I wasn't a meteorologist by any means, but it looked like rain was in the forecast. The waves were rougher than they'd been earlier, and it took a lot of energy just to make it beyond the break.

After taking a deep breath, I made the first of many dives down to the boat. It took several trips, but I managed to retrieve a few more cans of fruit cocktail, tuna and a bottle of cheap chardonnay. Silas's knife and one of the scuba tanks and a mask were the last of the salvageable items that I was able to retrieve from the boat.

Henryk and Viktor had been right to worry about me. I reached a new level of exhaustion after my last dive and collapsed on the wet sand. Viktor scooped me up and carried me to our makeshift camp-site, nestling me beside Silas under a layer of dry clothes for a blanket, while Henryk collected the small haul I'd piled on the beach.

It wasn't as much as I'd hoped, but it was enough to buy us a little more time.

# CHAPTER 14

## VIKTOR

Erin was strong willed and sexy as sin, but she'd taken one hell of a risk swimming out to the boat that many times. I tried to make a case for Henryk or me to make the dive, but she refused to listen to reason. It was more than a little obvious that that was one argument I wasn't going to win. Sure, she'd found a few cans of food, but at what cost? Silas was already laid up because of me. If something happened to her, I'd never forgive myself.

Still, as much as I wanted to be pissed at her for putting herself in harm's way, it was impossible when she looked so damned beautiful curled up next to Silas.

"Maybe we should head back up to the cabin. Have another look around while they're sleeping." I nodded toward Erin and Silas still resting near the smoldering fire.

"It couldn't hurt." Henryk grabbed a couple of the empty champagne bottles and tucked them under his arm. "I think there was an old well pump outside the cabin. If it works and the well hasn't run dry, we can bring some water back to camp."

"If it still looks like no one's home, maybe we can bring them to the cabin instead." As much as I hated to admit it, he was right.

Moving our camp from the beach to the cabin was our best shot at survival until we were rescued. And we would be rescued. Henryk was a prince. A member of the royal family of Liechtenstein doesn't just disappear off the face of the Earth. The king and queen—or at least the people they hired to search for him—would leave no stone unturned until they brought Henryk home.

Silas needed medical treatment. Worst case scenario, he faced a number of surgeries followed by physical therapy. Best case scenario, a cast and a heavy dose of antibiotics to fight off any infection in the open wounds. A tough diagnosis either way for a guy who spent his days on a construction site.

The weather on our deserted island had been mild. Ocean breezes kept the temperature and humidity down, but the sun had been brutal. We all suffered from sunburn. Erin never complained, but I saw the signs of blistering and peeling on her arms. The cabin would provide some much-needed shade, and if we were lucky, a little reprieve from the gnats and mosquitos that seemed to swarm at night.

"Shall we?" Henryk asked, once again allowing me to take the lead. Something he'd done a few times since we'd come to a truce back up at the cabin.

The prince and I had butted heads from day one, probably because I acted like a jackass most of the time where he was concerned. But I made a promise to work on it for Erin's sake. For all our sakes. Henryk was a little uptight, but he was a good guy. It was obvious he had genuine feelings for Erin. For Silas and me too. And if I were being honest with myself, those feelings went both ways.

A relationship with four people wouldn't work if you only cared about one person in it.

I lightened his load, taking one of the glass bottles in order for him to keep one hand free for the climb, and headed for the path. The trip back up to the cabin was a hell of a lot easier the second time around. We knew what landmarks to look for and had worn a path through the overgrown underbrush covering the rainforest floor.

"I think I saw a pump around the back side of the cabin." Henryk stepped out from behind me once we reached the clearing and walked around to the far side of the building while I hung back and examined the rest of the surrounding property.

Once I was sure the only set of prints were the ones we'd left the day before, I met him around back to check out the well pump.

"A little rusty but probably not enough for it to be seized up." I tugged on the handle, but it wouldn't budge. "Then again, I could be wrong."

"If we only had some lubricating oil." Henryk studied the pump completely unaware of the hilarity of what he'd just said.

Silas wasn't there to make the joke, so the burden fell on me. "That's what she said."

It took a moment for the prince to catch on, but once he did, his laughter was contagious.

"Oh, my stomach hurts from laughing so much." He wiped the tears from the corners of his eyes and doubled over. "I needed that."

"Me, too. The laughs have been a little short in supply these days." My mood had darkened over the last couple of days, and I wasn't the only one. It was hard to be upbeat all the time, especially with the severity of our situation weighing down on us. "Grab that small log over there. We'll give this thing a couple of whacks, see if we can't knock some of the rust off and free the handle up."

Henryk, seeming to need a way to let out his pent-up frustrations, grabbed the log and smacked the hell out of the well pump.

"Whoa, that ought to do it. We're not trying to break the thing." I grabbed the log before he could whack it again and chucked the wood off to the side. "Care to do the honors?"

"It's an interesting shade of beige, but that could be from lack of use and not contamination." Henryk raised and lowered the handle, priming the pump until a fresh—or mostly fresh—stream of water poured from the spout.

With the pump primed and the water flowing, he cupped his hands beneath the stream and brought it to his mouth.

"Hang on a sec." I took hold of his wrist and tugged his hands away from his face. "I think we should boil it just to be safe."

I was already responsible for the disastrous situation we were in.

The last thing I needed was to be responsible for his royal highness getting a case of dysentery.

"Yes, of course, you're right." Henryk used the hem of his shirt to dry his hands. "I got carried away with the excitement of a reliable fresh water source."

"Hey, I get it. I was getting used to the taste of champagne and caviar myself, but right now, fresh water beats just about anything. Let's take another look around and see if there's anything useful we missed last time and then head back to the beach."

"With any luck, Silas will be feeling up to making the trip up here tomorrow." Henryk walked around to the front of the cabin and onto the porch.

"I hope so. I really do. It's killing me seeing him laid up like that."

Silas was like my family, the closest thing I had to a brother, and my business partner. We shared everything. The highs, the lows. Even women. When he hurt, I hurt.

Henryk clasped his hand on my shoulder and gave me a comforting squeeze. "I'm sure his condition will improve once we get him off the beach, properly dress his wound and get him resting in an actual bed."

I hoped like hell he was right, because if Silas' condition got any worse, I didn't even want to think about what could happen. I'd never forgive myself.

We were more thorough with our second search of the cabin and found a few items we'd overlooked the other day, including an old ham radio. Which, much to our disappointment, was broken. At least in my opinion. Henryk seemed convinced he could fix it with the right equipment. Electronics weren't my thing, but we couldn't just order the parts we needed online, and the odds of them laying around somewhere were pretty slim.

We did find one small silver lining, however. A tri-fold pamphlet caught between the track and the underside of a drawer in the kitchen that advertised the island paradise and the reality TV show that had been filmed there a few years ago.

"I caught a couple of episodes of this. It used to air during the time slot before Sunday Night Football." I glanced around the cabin, counting off the square footage in my head. "Man, this place looked a lot nicer and a hell of a lot bigger on TV."

"It's all camera angles and lighting." Henryk flipped through the brochure. "Their ratings must have been reflected in their budget. Based on this, the show only ran for two seasons. But the good news is this isn't an uncharted island. We're still on the map."

"Yeah, now we just need to get back on the grid."

Something that was a hell of a lot easier said than done. Still, it was a glimmer of hope. Something to lift Erin, Henryk and Silas' spirits to get them through another day. I, on the other hand, wasn't going to get my hopes up. I wasn't born a pessimist, life made me that way. Growing up, the glass was always half empty, usually because someone drank out of it first. It was the hard way, all the way, but I learned the value of hand-me-downs over handouts and hard work.

Just because our island was charted didn't mean we knew the coordinates or had a way to give them to anyone. There was a lot of blue on a map, and I doubted if even the royal family had the resources to search all of it.

# CHAPTER 15

## HENRYK

*Day 4*

Based on the number of sunrises and sunsets, we were on our fourth day stranded on the island. It might as well have been four months, or four years, for that matter. Still, I took comfort in the fact that while our island may have been deserted, it wasn't uncharted. It belonged to someone. Whether that be an individual, a corporation or a country, somewhere out there, someone knew this place existed.

And that significantly increased our odds of being found.

In the meantime, we had a place to take shelter. We had a means of sustainable fresh water, and the ocean would provide enough food for all of us... assuming we could catch it. It felt like things were looking up, at least for the time being. Moods and situations changed as frequently as the tides, I understood, and shared in my friends' frustrations.

Viktor and I were finally on the same page, and it was time to break camp on the beach and move up to the cabin. There was just one obstacle to overcome if we were going to get what little supplies we had packed up and make the trek before nightfall. It was a fifteen-minute hike through the rainforest to reach the cabin, less if the trail was maintained. A task that I planned to tackle as soon as we were situated, making our trips down to the beach to tend the signal fires that much easier. Overgrowth wasn't the problem, however.

Silas' injury was.

He couldn't make the walk on his own, and hoisting him over one of our shoulders or onto our backs would make for a slow, arduous trip. We needed to fashion a gurney or a sled out of the supplies at hand, namely tree limbs and palm leaves.

Viktor was a contractor and craftsman, good with his hands and no doubt more than capable of making a gurney. But without any tools at his disposal, constructing one became a whole lot more complicated and took the better part of the day.

Erin busied herself with packing the last of our canned goods, along with the clothing from a piece of luggage she found washed up on the beach, into the suitcase. The sun had settled lower in the sky, signaling it was well past noon by the time our preparations for the hike were completed. But to my relief, we had plenty of daylight hours left to get up to the cabin and get settled.

"Look, you guys." Erin pointed to the surf and a shiny black object partially buried in the wet sand. "I think it's another suitcase."

She ran off to collect it, digging it out of the compacted sand, while Viktor and I waited with Silas at the opening of the trail.

"There wasn't much in there. Mostly clothes. I think they're yours, Silas. There are also a few toiletries, though I'm not sure how good any of them will be after soaking in salt water for so long." She held the suitcase's handle in a death grip despite not being overly impressed with its contents.

"I'm sure we can find a use for everything, and the toiletries may feel like a luxury when you see the bathroom in the cabin."

"I hope you're using the word bathroom loosely, because from what you've described, it barely meets the requirements of indoor plumbing," Erin teased, but there was some truth in her joke.

The cabin had a sink, shower and tub, thanks to the well. What it did not have was a functioning toilet. There was an outhouse. In the short time we had been stranded on the island, we learned first-hand how underappreciated and taken for granted a toilet was when compared with other modern conveniences.

"Hey, talk to me about an outhouse when you have to get someone to carry you to the woods," Silas quipped, making light of the severity of his injuries.

"Well, it's kind of hard to argue with that." Erin shook her head and smiled.

"The water for the shower feeds into the pipes through a storage tank where it's warmed by the sun, and we can boil water for hot baths." Viktor gave his best sales pitch on the few amenities the cabin did have.

"Are you sure you're a contractor and not a realtor?" Erin laughed as she jostled the suitcases and adjusted her grip on the handles. "Honestly, though, a bath sounds amazing."

"I'm sure that can be arranged." With any luck, that bathtub was big enough for two, and I could join her. "In fact, after we get Silas comfortable, I will make it my first priority."

"It doesn't need to be the first or even third priority." Erin moved off to the side when she reached the end of the trail to make room for Viktor and me to pass through with the gurney carrying Silas. "We have a lot of work to do from the looks of it."

"This isn't our forever home. How bad can it be?" Silas chuckled and craned his neck over the side of the stretcher for his first glimpse of the cabin. "Uh, forget I asked."

"Well, it's no private bungalow on the beach of Ibiza, but I'm sure we can all make do." Viktor balanced the stretcher with one hand and opened the bedroom door. "At least you get the bed."

"Silver linings, huh?" Silas pressed his palms on the mattress and hoisted himself off the stretcher while Erin propped pillows to support his injured leg. "If I have to be bedridden, at least the company is good."

The corners of Erin's mouth turned upward, curving her full lips into a smile as she beamed at him. I had a castle, untold wealth, the future of an entire nation in my hands, but I would have traded it all for one look from her like that. Self-sacrifice was something my parents had drilled into me from a young age, and yet sharing Erin was harder than I would have expected.

Still, she was worth the effort, and I would take her any way that I could get her.

With Silas settled and resting in the bedroom, Viktor, Erin and I went to organize what remained of our supplies.

"We don't have much food left. There's maybe enough for two meals, if we're lucky." Erin took the canned goods from the table and restacked them on the kitchen counter. "We've got the water covered, and that buys us some more time, but we don't know how long a rescue is going to take, so we're going to have to do something about food."

"And fast." Viktor rubbed his growling stomach and glanced back at the bedroom where his best friend lay sleeping. "I'm starving already, and Silas definitely needs more calories for his body to heal."

"We only had enough time for a cursory search of the cabin when we discovered it." I folded one of the piles of clothes we sorted from Silas' suitcase and set it on the wicker loveseat in the living area. "Perhaps we missed something."

"Well, we know the kitchen's empty." Viktor pushed himself off the side of the counter where he'd propped himself and walked toward the front door. "Why don't you and Erin see if there's anything useful hiding in here. The brush is pretty overgrown out there. Maybe there's a shed or a generator or something hiding in the palm trees."

"It shouldn't take us too long to comb over the cabin. Henryk and I will come out and give you a hand once we're done." Erin walked Viktor out and closed the door behind him. "Okay, I'll start in the bedroom. You see what you can find out here."

"Why do you get to the search the bedroom?" I teased.

"Don't be jealous, your highness." She giggled, picked up one of the folded shirts from my pile on the wicker seat and chucked it at my head. "Silas is resting, and I'm a lot quieter than you or Viktor."

"You make a valid point." I closed the distance between us, encircling my arms around her tiny waist, pulled her close and brushed a kiss against her lips. "Good luck in your search."

"Good luck to you too." She wrapped her arms around me and deepened the kiss enough for me to yearn for something more before she pulled away.

The woman was a snake charmer, entrancing me with the natural sway of her hips as she turned and walked into the bedroom. I considered calling off the search of the cabin and surrounding grounds for supplies or survival items in lieu of another risqué rendezvous with all three of my so-called exes. There was no doubt in my mind that this had to be the most bizarre divorce proceedings in the history books.

Still, I wouldn't change a thing.

Except perhaps the actual divorce. From the moment the three of them convinced me to take a vacation with them, I have been reevaluating my life and the things I want. Or don't want, a marriage to Posey being top among them. I was a prince of Liechtenstein, the royal heir, and had all the luxuries of life. Save one.

My freedom.

With that depressing thought, I gave up the notion of losing myself in the only place I had ever found true happiness—in the arms of Erin, Silas, and Viktor. It was selfish of me to want them so badly when I knew it would never work out. Not the way it should or in the way they deserved. All three of them had fulfilling lives, friends, families, and careers to return to. They needed to be rescued.

And I needed to forget about a future with them in it. This was one story where the prince would not get his happily ever after.

I fought my way through the melancholy along with several spider webs and a massive layer of dust and took a deep dive into the hall closet. Upon first glance, its contents appeared to be the same as when Viktor and I first searched the cabin, until I looked up at the ceiling. There was something unusual about one of the wooden panels. A notch cut out in the side large enough for my finger to fit into. I stuck my thumb in the notch and pressed my fingertips against the panel to pop it out of place.

*An access panel.*

Perhaps there was something useful stored above the closet in what I assumed was an attic space. With the panel propped against the back wall, I reached up in the opening and hoisted myself up. It opened to a small, narrow attic space that ran the length of the cabin's peaked roof. With the open design and vaulted ceiling, I never gave attic storage much thought. There was no electric and only minimal plumbing, which ran through a crawl space beneath the cabin. An attic would have been unnecessary.

Unless, of course, you were using it to hide a TV camera for a reality show.

If that was the real reason it had been incorporated into the cabin's design, I was grateful to the production team, because they'd left behind more than one useful item. Not only were there two fishing poles, which would hopefully provide a much-needed protein source and get us a lot closer to a reasonable caloric intake than the sparse rations we had left, there was also a lantern with a full pot of kerosene.

But most importantly, a satellite phone.

The battery was dead, and the antenna was loose, but with a little luck and a lot of ingenuity, those were two problems that I could fix.

I had an idea. One that just might save our lives… if it didn't kill me first.

# CHAPTER 16

## ERIN

"You must be severely dehydrated or have sun poisoning or something." I raked my fingers through my hair, snagging them in the salt crusted, tangled ends. "Because if you think I'm going to let you go dive down and search the wreckage for some black box thing, you have clearly lost your mind."

"Erin, please be reasonable about this." Henryk reached for me, but I stepped out of arms' length.

"I realize you grew up in a castle and everything, so this may be news to you, but insinuating that a woman is unreasonable is not a good way to win an argument." I rested one hand on my hip and stabbed the air with my pointer finger of the other hand for emphasis. "Quite the opposite. In fact, it's a fast track from the bedroom to the couch."

"Hey, go easy on him." Silas pressed his palms against the mattress and pushed, inching himself up the headboard to an upright position. "That's not what he meant."

His raised hands and the defeated look in his eyes took the wind right out of my sails when I rounded on him. Silas and Henryk were right. I *was* being unreasonable, but I couldn't help it. My nerves were getting the best of me, and if something happened to Henryk, I would never forgive myself.

"I know." I wrapped my arms around my midsection and pushed out a long breath. "I shouldn't have snapped at you, Henryk. It's just... I worry. I can't help it. If you got hurt or—"

"It's all right." Henryk closed the distance between us and pulled me into his arms. "How do you think we felt watching you dive over and over again for supplies until you were so exhausted you collapsed on the beach? At least I'll just be going down once."

"You say that like it's supposed to make me feel better." I nuzzled into this chest and allowed myself to relax in the security of his arms, if only for a moment. "At least wait until the storm passes. The wind is picking up, and I'm sure the waves are too."

"Under normal circumstances I would agree that waiting out the weather would be the best thing to do, but we don't know how stable the wreckage is. Stronger waves and a stronger current could make things more difficult after the storm passes." Henryk's muscles tensed as if he were bracing against another argument from me as well as the first crack of thunder outside.

"Where there's thunder, there's lightning." I pushed out of our embrace and rested my hands on my hips. "It's not safe to be in the water when there's lightning. So, that settles it. You're waiting until after the storm passes."

"I need to do this. We all need me to do this, Erin." Henryk walked toward the bedroom door, stopping to glance back over his shoulder. "I won't be long. I promise."

"You're not going to try and talk some sense into him?" I looked to Silas for back-up, but he must have had the good sense not to take sides because he just shook his head. "Fine. There's still one person left who's more stubborn than you. If you won't listen to me, maybe you'll listen to him. Viktor?"

"Good luck *with that*," Silas chuckled, batting at the wadded-up ball of socks I pulled from the suitcase and tossed at his head.

"Viktor, I need your help!" I called out as I squeezed between

Henryk and the doorjamb and stormed out into the living area. "Viktor?"

The cabin was smaller than my apartment back home and had little privacy or places to hide. Viktor would have heard Henryk and me arguing, and there's no way he wouldn't have heard me calling for him. Panic gripped my heart.

"He's not here?" I asked without bothering to wait for an answer before rushing toward the front door and yanking it open. "Viktor?"

"He was going to check around the cabin for a generator or any other equipment left behind by the film crew that we might be able to use." Henryk was already by my side as I stepped onto the porch. "He's probably around the back of the cabin."

"Viktor!" I charged down the steps and sprinted around the side of the house, calling after him as I went. "He's not here."

Henryk caught up to me at the back of the cabin and joined my search of the surrounding tree line. We pushed further into the rainforest, calling out to Viktor, but there was no sign of him anywhere.

"Where could he have gone?" I grabbed Henryk's hand and led him back inside. As much as I didn't want to worry Silas in his condition, we needed to tell him that Viktor had gone missing.

Henryk slowed his pace, jerking my arm when he came to a full stop at the kitchen table. "The knife. The one you gave him, it's gone."

"What?" I stared at the empty tabletop, trying to recall if the knife had been there or if Henryk had been mistaken. "Are you sure you saw it before?"

"Yes, I'm positive. I noticed it after he went to look for a generator and planned to ask him if I could borrow it before I left to go down to the wreck. I thought it might be useful." Henryk brushed his fingertips across the table before pressing his palm against the wooden surface, as if marking the spot where the knife had been. "You don't suppose he—"

"Went down to the beach to dive for the black box?" I pressed my hands to my mouth, stifling the gasp of air before it escaped my lips.

"If I know Viktor, and believe me, I know him better than he knows himself," Silas chimed in, joining the conversation from where he still rested on the bed. "That's exactly where he went."

"Silas, I'm sorry." I crossed the living area and stood in the doorway. "I didn't mean to worry you. I'm sure everything's fine. Viktor's fine, right Henryk?"

I spared a glance over my shoulder at Henryk, hoping he would offer the same reassurances. Which I needed to hear as much as Silas did. Probably more so, if I were honest.

"Of course, he is. Viktor is more than capable of handling himself." Henryk moved up behind me, nodding his affirmation.

"So, we're not worried about the storm that's about to pummel us, or the lightning and thunder cracking outside anymore?" Silas crossed his arms over his chest, eyes narrowing as he watched both of us from across the room.

"What? Oh, my gosh, that's not what I meant. Of course, I'm worried." Tears burned my eyes, blurring my vision and threatening to spill over my lashes onto my cheeks. "I just don't want you to worry. Not in your condition. It's not like you can just run after him, knock some sense into him and drag him back to the cabin."

"And you can?" Silas's arched brow matched the upturned curve on the left side of his mouth.

"Well, I'm damn sure going to try." I looped my arm through Henryk's, offering his assistance in the search and rescue mission. "We both are."

"Hang on, there." Silas combed his hair back out of his face. "That is not what I meant, and you know it. I'm worried as much as you are. Probably more, actually. I mean, he's the closest thing I have to a brother. Which means, I also know there is no knocking any sense into him when he's got his mind made up about something. I also know the same reasons you were worried about Henryk going down to the beach apply to you."

"I can't just sit here and do nothing, Silas." My stomach roiled and twisted into knots. "It's too dangerous. If we leave now, we can catch up to him on the trail or down at the beach before he hits the water. He'll listen to me. He has to."

"Erin, do you hear that?" Silas jerked his thumb toward the window and the black clouds outside the window. "The wind is howling and those heavy plunks on the roof are some big-ass raindrops. The sky is about to open up. The only thing we can do now is hunker down and wait for him to come back."

"It's not that bad yet." I watched the shadows shift and merge together as the last of the sun's rays that beamed through the window were swallowed up by the storm clouds. "There's enough time to get Viktor and get back before the worst of it hits us."

"So you're a meteorologist now?" Silas' meager smile did little to hide the worry reflected in his eyes. "Take another look at that storm out there, Erin. It's just like the one that capsized the boat and marooned us on this island. As much as I want you in this bed beside me, I don't want it to be because you got hurt chasing after Viktor. And neither would he."

"I have to try, Silas." I blew him a kiss and pushed past Henryk. "If the weather starts to get really bad, I'll turn back. I promise. But I have to at least try."

Before either of them could argue, I dashed out of the bedroom and across the living room to the front door. The moment I turned the doorknob, releasing the latch, a strong gust of wind ripped it from my hands. The hinges were bent, the frame cracked and there was a circular indentation in the wall the exact size of the doorknob.

The storm had arrived.

Rain pelted the cabin, soaking the doormat and puddling up on the cupped and worn floorboards. Thunder boomed overhead, rattling my heart along with the cabin, Lightning flashed across the sky.

There was a crack followed by a large crash and an eruption of sparks in the trees across the small clearing around the front of the house. Lightning had struck a tree and started a small brush fire.

There was no way I could make it down to the beach in weather like that, and no way that I could stop Viktor. He was out there by himself, in the elements, with nowhere to take shelter. Which was one of the reasons we all decided to leave the beach and head to the cabin in the first place. He obviously heard my argument with Henryk and decided to take matters into his own hands, resolving it the only way he knew how.

"The rain will keep the fire from spreading." Henryk rested his hand on my shoulder and steered me back into the living room. "Erin, I know you want to blame yourself for Viktor being out there right now, but it's not your fault. If anyone is to blame, it's me. It was my idea to go back to the boat and search for the black box."

"Am I that predictable?" I let out a breath, brushed my bangs out of my eyes and tucked the stray hairs behind my ear.

"Not in the way you might think." Henryk caught my hand and clasped it in his, resting them both on his chest above his heart. "I knew you would feel that way because of how deeply you care. You've shown that side of yourself to me, to all of us. It's who you are."

I stretched up on tiptoes, tilted my head to one side and pressed my lips to his in a tender kiss. "If this isn't my fault, then it isn't yours either. Looking for the black box was a good idea. I just wish Viktor had said something before he left. We could have gone with him. Now he's out there by himself. What if he tried to make the dive and got caught out in the open water in the storm? What if he's hurt? Or worse, what if he's…"

The words stuck in my throat. I couldn't bring myself to think of something happening to Viktor. Or any of them, for that matter. There was nothing I could do but wait and hope that he made it back to us, because now that I had him, I couldn't imagine my life without Viktor in it. His absence proved that.

The real problem was how I was going to keep him and Silas and Henryk once we were rescued.

# CHAPTER 17

## SILAS

My leg was fucking killing me, but the pain I felt from my injuries was nothing compared to the pain I felt knowing Erin was hurting too. The only problem was her wounds weren't on the outside. There was no bandage or tourniquet that I could put on her heart.

Viktor had the only remedy she needed.

I just wish I knew when the hell he'd be back with the medicine that we all needed. Because truth be told, I could do with a dose of Viktor myself. He was more than my business partner, he was my best friend. We shared everything. Work, women, life. If something happened to him while I was laid up in a damned bed, I would never forgive myself. He shouldn't have been out there, not without me helping him.

Erin came into the room, her eyes all puffy and red from crying, and collapsed on the bed beside me. She sniffled away the last of her tears as she curled up beside me and rested her head on my shoulder.

"Hey, it's going to be all right." I ran my hand through her hair, twirling a strand around the end of my fingers. "Viktor's stubborn as hell, and a little hot-headed at times, but he's not stupid. He's not going to put himself in danger. Not when he's got you to come back to. Trust me."

"You think so?" She used the sleeve of my shirt to dab the corners of her eyes.

"I don't think so, I know so." I brushed my lips across her forehead. "Because Viktor and I are one in the same. And if it were me down there on the beach, the only thing I would be thinking about is you."

"Everyone acts like I'm this perfect, precious thing." She sniffled again, choking on her words as she fought back another round of tears. "But I'm not. I'm selfish."

"Selfish?" I trailed my fingers down her arm, following it down where it draped over her ribs, and brushed my thumb along the underside of her breast. "I hate to disagree with you, sweetheart, but you are far from selfish. You're the most generous lover Viktor and I have ever been with. You've given a piece of yourself to all of us."

"That's not what I'm talking about, and you know it." She slid her hand over my chest and traced the planes of my stomach with her fingertips. "This was supposed to be a fling, nothing permanent, but I don't want it to end. I don't want to choose one or even two of you. I want to keep all of you in my life. Forever. If that's not selfish, then what is? I mean, you and Viktor have this amazing opportunity to expand your construction business with that new contract. Henryk has an entire country and I have my dream job offer back in New Jersey. But all I can think about is the three of you."

"What dream job?" I rested my hand on hers, stilling the nervous circles she drew with her fingers along my ribs. "You never mentioned a promotion or anything."

"My boss called before we left the dock." Erin tilted her head back and looked up at me. "There didn't seem to be any point in bringing it up. I mean, we're all supposed to go our separate ways after this, so a new job for me didn't really matter. But the more I'm with all of you, the more I realize that all the things I have back home, my job, my apartment…none of that matters without all of you in my life."

"It's not selfish to know what you want in life and to go after it. Especially when you're not hurting anyone in the process. I can't speak for Henryk because his situation is... well, it's pretty unbeliev-able. He's a prince, for cripes sake. But Viktor and me, we'll figure it out."

"Silas, I don't think you understand." Erin's sapphire eyes sparkled through the tears that spilled over her lashes. "I love you. I'm in love with you."

My heart stopped, and the breath in my lungs hitched in my throat when she gave voice to the feelings that I had but was too afraid to admit. I'd fallen in love with Erin somewhere between Liechtenstein and our deserted island. I wanted her more than I wanted anything in my life, and I would do whatever it took to keep her. There was no doubt in my mind that Viktor felt the same.

But from the look on the prince's face, Henryk would be a little harder to convince.

He'd made his way to the bedroom, lingering in the doorway long enough to overhear and completely misunderstand what Erin meant.

"I'm in love with all three of you. That's impossible, isn't it?" Erin choked back a sob and wiped the back of her hand across her eyes. "My heart feels like it's full to bursting whenever I'm in the room with you, Viktor and Henryk. I don't want just one of you. *I need all of you.*"

Henryk had turned his back to us, no doubt ready to retreat behind the formalities of his title and upbringing but stilled at her words. I watched the tension ease from his shoulders and knew the moment he realized that he was included. That Erin loved him too.

"Is it really true? What you said about loving all of us?" Henryk turned and gripped the doorjamb, bracing himself for a moment before he crossed the bedroom and perched himself on the corner of the mattress.

"Of course, it is." Erin stretched her arm, inviting the prince to join us further up on the mattress. "I wouldn't have said it if I didn't mean it."

"Say it again." Henryk stretched out behind her and wrapped his arm around her, his fingers brushing against me in the process. "I need to hear you say it."

"I love you, Henryk." Erin turned to him, claiming his mouth with hers in a deep and passionate kiss.

He pulled back and rested his forehead against hers. "I never thought I would fall in love. It wasn't part of the royal plans for me, but you changed all that. You changed me, Erin."

"I need all of you more than I have needed anything in my entire life."

She clung to us, and we held her tightly, fear for Viktor locking us in an embrace that was impossible to break.

# CHAPTER 18

## VIKTOR

The scuba tank and mask were still on the beach, right where Erin had left them, which saved me precious time that, based on the look of the blackened sky, I didn't have. Another storm was rolling in off the ocean, and it looked to be worse than the one that stranded us here.

It was a now or never, do or die situation.

The tide was already moving in and the whitecaps on the water meant it was rougher than hell. It would take a lot of strength and energy to make it past the break and fight the current to get down to the wreck. If I wasn't careful, I wouldn't have enough left in the tank to make it back to the surface with the black box.

Assuming I found the damned thing to begin with.

Henryk hadn't exactly been forthcoming with its location during his argument with Erin. Although, I hadn't stuck around long enough to find out if he divulged any more details, either. All I knew was that we needed the black box and the batteries inside it to fix the radio and call for help.

And that was all the information I needed to know.

Erin and Henryk could have stood around and argued about who should make the dive until the sea levels rose enough from global warming to turn the cabin from a waterfront view to a waterfront property. There was too much talking and not enough action for me. It was time to get shit done.

Henryk had no business diving down to the wreckage, anyway. Erin had been right about that. He was a prince, a living heir, and there was already enough social and political bullshit within the royal family. We did not need to add an injured prince—or worse—to our list of problems with the king and queen of Liechtenstein.

They'd probably have Ray hire some freelance mercenary, black ops wetwork team to take us out. I mean, a few dead tourists? We wouldn't be more than a blip on the nightly news. Forgotten between the six and eleven o'clock broadcasts. There were only a handful of people who would probably miss me, and they were all there on the island with me.

I strapped the tank on my back, pulled the mask over my head and waded out past the break in the water until I was chest deep and my toes were still able to touch bottom, then dove through the barrel of the next cresting wave. It took three or four more tries to make it far enough out to actually dive down to the wreck without getting knocked back onto the beach.

The water was clear enough to see the bottom of the ocean floor and the boat. It had capsized, just like Erin said. Not that I doubted her, but I was hoping she was wrong. The boat being upside down made my search for its hidden compartments that much more complicated.

Based on what I'd overheard Henryk explain to Erin, the box wasn't out in the open with the rest of the controls in the wheelhouse, or whatever the hell they called it on a yacht. Henryk no doubt knew the right word, given his fancy pants education. It was difficult, but I tried not to blame him for that. Henryk couldn't change being brought up in a palace any more than I could a foster home. They were the cards we were dealt, and we had no choice but to play them out.

It was a shame the prince couldn't cash out though. Things wouldn't be the same for Erin without him. It was pretty clear she had feelings for him—for all of us—and I wasn't sure how she was going to cope when this all came to an end, and we were forced to say our goodbyes. At least to Henryk. Because I didn't plan on saying anything of the sort to Erin.

There was no way in hell I was walking away from her.

I found a toolbox under the sink in the yacht's small galley kitchen. Most of the tools were useless when it came to removing a black box underwater. I grabbed the screwdriver, a claw hammer and a multi-tool that might come in handy when I made it back to the cabin. There wasn't enough air left in the tank to search the entire ship. I needed to stay focused and concentrate on the areas most likely to contain the device. Tools in hand, I swam out of the kitchen and turned my focus to the bridge.

There weren't any nails to pry out, but the claw hammer came in handy prying off the plastic housing that covered the steering mecha-nism. No black box, or at least not that I could tell. I wasn't entirely sure what I was looking for, and there were several black, plastic, water-tight covers underneath the main housing to protect smaller parts from saltwater damage in the event of a breach in the hull.

Sinking to the bottom of the ocean, not so much.

The damage was done, and the yacht was a total loss. Water seeped through every nook and cranny. There wasn't an air bubble left inside the cabin, and I was running out of time. I moved on to a new section, prying back plastic covers and snapping the clips that held them in place until I finally found what I was looking for. Or at least, I hoped I did.

The black box was larger and heavier than I anticipated, making for a difficult swim back to the surface. My hamstrings burned from the excessive amount of kicking required to compensate for a one-handed stroke and I was in danger of running out of air before I reached the surface. Still, the seal for the compartment in the recorder that contained the precious batteries Henryk needed to fix the satel-lite phone appeared to be intact.

I drew the last breath of air from the tank and held it for as long as possible, sucking in a mouthful of saltwater into my lungs as I broke the surface. It tasted like shit, set my chest on fire and caused a coughing fit that left me dry heaving by the time I reached the beach.

But at least I made it to the beach, and I still had the black box.

Something I wasn't sure the prince could have done if Erin let him go in the first place. He was fit enough to make the dive and swim down to the boat, but the actual retrieval would have been a problem. Henryk didn't strike me as the type of guy who spent a lot of time with a screwdriver and a hammer. I worked construction, spent the better part of my days with a tool in each hand, which made me the perfect man for the job.

If I was lucky, I could convince Erin of that when I got back. I supposed it was better to ask forgiveness than permission. She'd have a hard time staying mad at me when I made it back to the cabin with the black box in hand. Or at least, that's what I hoped.

All that was left to do was make it to the cabin. A feat that looked more difficult with each passing second. The wind picked up, battering the palm trees lining the beach with near hurricane force gusts, and the roiling water pulled the sand from the shore back down to the ocean depths. If the storm didn't let up, there wouldn't be anywhere for a rescue ship to beach once Henryk made the call.

The smart move would have been to find somewhere to take shelter in the rainforest near the beach. Good thing no one had ever accused me of being smart. As Silas liked to say, I was all brawn and no brains. Well, at least I was smart enough to find the box and save our asses.

After all, the greater the risk, the greater the reward. And I could think of a few rewards available on our deserted island that were worth the effort.

The trail back to the cabin had been washed out by runoff from the storm's massive rainfall, making the climb up to the structure treacherous. I stuck to the tree line, using palms that hadn't been snapped in half by the battering winds for support. When the cabin's pitched roof came into view, I was gasping for breath and clutching a coconut tree just to stay upright.

I used the last of my strength to crawl up the porch steps and tossed the black box beside the door. Bringing it inside had to wait until I caught my breath. I collapsed on the porch and rolled to my side, tucking in against the side of the cabin as much as possible to stay out of the pelting rain. Sleep would have claimed me right there if not for Erin.

"Viktor? Is that you?" Erin called out. Her voice was small against the sound of the wind and rain hammering the side of the cabin, but the urgency came through loud and clear. "Oh, thank you, God."

Adrenaline coursed through my veins. I pushed myself up to my feet and rushed inside. The kitchen and living room were empty. That left the bedroom. Silas was in there. My heart hammered in my chest. Had his condition worsened while I was gone? Was he unconscious? What if I missed my last chance to talk to him while I was out getting the stupid fucking box? A million horrible scenarios raced through my mind in the few seconds it took me to reach the bedroom, but the scene in front of me was nothing like I imagined.

The three of them were laying on the bed, clinging to each other. Erin was in the center, sitting up and staring at me with big eyes. "Are you okay?"

I nodded, walking into the room. They were all clothed, but I could feel the intensity in the room. The electricity pulsing around all of us.

Erin bit her lip. "We waited for you."

I began to strip off my clothes, needing them now. "Start. I wanna watch." And when I was dry, I'd join them.

* * *

SILAS

NOW THAT VIKTOR WAS BACK, and he was safe, I had a million questions. But Erin had other plans. She rolled onto her back and reached for my hand, placing it between her legs. Then she took Henryk's and rubbed it on her breast.

Erin was being a complete wanton, and she knew Viktor was watching. She arched her back, a small moan escaping her lips when I slipped my fingers between the crotch of her shorts and tugged at the hem of her panties. Erin wasted no time unfastening my shorts and working them down past my hips. Her hands trembled with need, but she was careful to avoid jostling my leg.

Henryk joined in, stripping off his clothes along with Erin's and helped ease her into position. I never shied away from a little pleasure and pain, but my leg was a different story, and I appreciated the care they put into taking care of *all my needs*.

Erin straddled my hips and held onto my cock before she slid down and buried the full length inside her. She was hot, wet and tight. Everything about Erin drove me fucking crazy. I gripped her hips, slowing her grinding before she pushed me over the edge, and I came to an end before things really got started.

Henryk positioned himself between my legs, and pressed Erin down until her soft, perfect breasts were mashed against my chest. He licked his fingers and ran them between her slick pussy and her ass, lubing her up to take her from behind.

"Yes, oh, God. Yes," Erin moaned in my ear. "This is what I want, what I need. Fuck me, please."

I groaned and dug my fingers into her ass cheeks, holding on tight as Henryk rode her ass and used the momentum to slide Erin's pussy up and down my dick. She was so tight, so full with both of us inside her and the sensation of Henryk and me fucking her at the same time was driving me wild.

Erin called out to Viktor, naked now. "Viktor? Please join us."

Viktor shook his head and smiled. "No. Keep going."

She cried out at the pleasure, the exquisite torture of being filled to the brim. She pulled back, then thrust down again, deep, hard, and powerful. She turned my head, sobbing from the bliss, and begged for more.

"You like that?" Erin nipped at my ear, sucking the lobe between her teeth. "You like feeling Henryk's dick in my ass, fucking me, while your hard cock is buried in my pussy?"

*Shit.* Our little princess had come a long way with the dirty talk, and if she kept it up, I wouldn't last. I gripped her hips hard and stopped her mid grind. "Easy, baby. I don't want this to be over too soon. I want to feel your pussy throb on my dick when I come."

"Silas, please." She begged for more and bit her lip when I held her in place.

Henryk buried himself in her ass and waited for me to ease my grip and let Erin move again.

I needed this, needed them as much as they needed me. As good as this felt, as much as I wanted to fill Erin's hot pussy with my cum, it wasn't the same without Viktor. We weren't complete without him, and I knew at that moment any future we had must have all four of us in it.

Erin, Henryk, Viktor and me. The thought of this kind of pleasure, this level of intimacy every day for the rest of my life, was enough to push me over the edge, but I held out. Held on to build the climax for Erin.

I wanted to give her something she would never forget, because as much as I wanted forever, I couldn't help but think this might be one of the last times we experienced this.

# CHAPTER 19

## VIKTOR

My dick was rock-hard, my balls tight and the only woman who could give me the release I needed was right there looking sexy as sin and getting fucked on the mattress in front of me.

Erin glanced back over her shoulder and fixed those shimmering sapphire eyes on me and pleaded with me to join them. I was all but gone.

There was no room for jealousy, not with her. Not when she was looking at me like that. After all, she had Silas' cock in her pussy, Henryk's in her ass, but it was my dick she was begging to taste, and I was more than happy to satisfy her desires.

I crossed the room, stripping off my soaked clothes as I went and stood beside the bed. I grabbed the base of my cock and slid my hand up and down in long, slow, intentional strokes until a bead of precum glistened on the tip.

"Is that what you want, baby?" I slid my hand back down, clamping my fingers around the base of my cock, relishing the throb as the cinched circulation increased the size and intensity of my erection. "That's right. That's what you fucking need, isn't it?"

Erin opened her mouth and flicked her tongue over the sensitive skin along the underside of the head of my dick before laving up the precum. She circled my dick with her lips, encasing it in the soft, wet heat of her marvelous mouth. Fuck, she was masterful when it came to sucking dick, and there was nothing sexier than watching her head bob up and down on my cock. Except maybe when she slowed to a stop and looked up at me with my dick balls deep in her mouth.

By the way she picked up the pace, pushed her hips back for Henryk as he pumped in and out of her ass while she rode each thrust on Silas's dick deep in her pussy, I knew she was close, so close to an orgasm ripping through her entire body. And it didn't take long for me to catch up. I dug my fingers in her hair, arched my back and tilted my hips until the head of my dick hit the back of her throat.

"Fuck, Erin." I eased out, sliding the length of my cock over her tongue as her orgasm ripped through her, ripping screams of pleasure from her throat while I shot my load on her mouth. She savored every drop, and I was still coming as she licked her lips and the head of my dick clean.

Henryk and Silas finished with us, each of them holding on to Erin as they rode the waves of their orgasms. Her skin, beaded with sweat, all but glowed as she collapsed on Silas's chest while Henryk took care to ease himself out and sprawled on the bed beside them. Erin rolled over him and patted the sliver of mattress left beside her.

"You think it will hold all of us?" I joked, wobbling on rubbery legs to the opposite side of the bed from where I stood.

"If the bed survived that, it can survive the four of us taking a nap." Erin held out her arms and waited for me to fall into them.

I thought about telling them about my successful dive and the black box out on the porch but couldn't bring myself to ruin the moment. There was no telling how many more we had left once Henryk fixed the sat phone and made the call to civilization.

The first rays of sun made their return through the bedroom window, warming my face and chasing away the last of the back clouds. The storm blew over and left sticky, oppressive heat behind. Sweat slicked my skin and soaked into the sheet beneath me. As much as I enjoyed the afterglow and the nap, it was too hot in the cabin to be trapped on the bed with all that added body heat.

"Are you alright, Viktor?" Henryk stirred when I wormed my way off the mattress and wiped the sleep from his eyes.

"Yeah, I'm good." It was a half-truth. I was good, but I was also dreading the conversation we were about to have because I feared it meant the end of some of the best days of my life. Which was crazy, considering how much trouble we'd had since we first left Liechtenstein. "I need to show you something."

I grabbed my shorts off the floor and hopped into them one foot at a time as I made my way out of the bedroom and out onto the porch. We were the closest we'd been to getting rescued. I should have been happy, but I wasn't. I was miserable. This was it. The beginning of the end. Our last days or hours together.

When we returned to Liechtenstein, we would say our last goodbyes.

# CHAPTER 20

## HENRYK

"Y%ou found it?" I could hardly contain my excitement when I saw the black box on the porch, but it was short lived when I realized what being rescued meant for my relationship with Erin, Viktor and Silas.

"Yeah, I had a hell of a time getting it out of the boat." Viktor rubbed the back of his neck with his hand, a physical tell that I had come to learn during our time together meant something was bothering him.

I suspected I knew what it was, because the same thing was bothering me. And no doubt Silas as well. Erin had expressed her feelings on the subject matter on more than one occasion. We all knew where she stood, and if my circumstances allowed it, I would have stood with her.

There were times in my life, especially when I was a young boy, that I fantasized about running away and leaving the titles, the crown and the responsibilities behind. But that's all they were. Fantasies. Until Erin, Viktor and Silas walked back into my life.

And I was going to have to walk away from them again, just like I had all those years ago on the blacktop of our childhood playground.

Once again, I would be left with nothing more than fantasies of *my happiness*, of my life outside of the crown and country. But these fantasies would not be those of a child's wishes, but a man's deepest desires. They would be born from the memories created over the past days and weeks spent with three veritable strangers who had become some of the most important people in my life.

"Thank you, Viktor." I bent down and picked up the black box, tucking it against my side to compensate for the added weight when I stood up. "It's a lot heavier than I expected. You know, Erin didn't want me to go. I tried to convince her that I could make the dive and retrieve the box with no problems. Now that I'm holding it in my hands, I'm not sure that I could have done it. Erin was terrified when you snuck off on your own. We all were, but you got it done. You were obviously the man for the job."

"The housing was a real bitch to get off, and I was running out of air. I thought I was going to have to leave without it, but it finally broke loose." Viktor pointed to the device in my hands. "Are you sure this will work? I mean, what if the batteries aren't compatible?"

"There's only one way to find out." I tamped down the doubts and hopes that I wouldn't be able to fix the satellite phone that battled for dominance in my head and brought the box inside.

"Is that it?" Erin finger combed her bedhead into submission as she shuffled out of the bedroom. "It's a lot bigger than I thought it would be. I can't believe you went out there by yourself, Viktor. What were you thinking?"

"That we needed it to fix the sat phone. We can't stay here forever, Erin. One more storm like the one we had yesterday, and this cabin is likely to blow over." Viktor misdirected Erin's concerns for his safety with a reminder that our little slice of island paradise wasn't paradise at all.

"I know, but you shouldn't have gone down there by yourself. What if something happened to you? Do you have any idea what that would have done to me?" Erin padded across the living room and wrapped her arms around Viktor, pulling him into a fierce embrace. "Viktor, I—"

"I know, Erin. I know." He stepped back and cupped her face in his hands. "I do too."

Fixing the satellite phone proved more difficult than I'd hoped. The batteries were compatible, but without a soldering iron, wire snips and precision screwdrivers, it was a tedious process. With the limited tools available at the cabin, it took several attempts before I was able to power up the phone.

"I think that should do it." I turned the power knob to the on position and held my breath.

"That's what you said the last time." Viktor's anticipation was palpable as he peered over my shoulder and examined my handiwork.

The bright green lights flickered, and a series of beeps came through the speaker as the batteries charged and brought the phone back to life.

"Hot damn, you did it." He slapped my shoulder and gave it a hearty squeeze. "I can't believe it. It's working."

"It's working, but do we have a signal?" Erin held the wires, stabilizing them as she held up the phone and checked the signal strength. "Oh my God, it is working. We have a signal. It's weak, but we have one. What's Ray's number?"

"Here, let me try." I took the phone, careful not to disrupt the loose wire connection and called the head of my security team. "Ray, can you hear me? Are you there?"

His voice squawked through the speaker. "Your Highness? Yes, yes. It's him. Shhh, I can't hear him with everyone talking at once."

I couldn't contain my amusement over Ray's ability to chastise my parents. He was one of the few people who dared to do so, and had done it on my behalf on more than one occasion.

"It's good to hear your voice, Ray." And it was. He was more than a bodyguard, he was my closest confidant, and with the best days of my life coming to an end, I would need him more than ever. "We need a medic. We were caught in a tropical storm and the yacht went down. Silas was injured. We did the best we could to tend to his wounds, but he needs a doctor's care."

"And the kidnappers? We received a ransom request for your return. Your parents were making arrangements for the payment, but communication stopped. We all feared the worst." Ray wouldn't let lack of contact with the kidnappers be the end of it. He was former military, highly skilled and chosen specifically by my parents to be in charge of my security detail. He would oversee our safe return to Liechtenstein and then oversee the manhunt for the men responsible for the kidnapping.

"They left us on the boat." Anger simmered beneath the surface. I wanted justice for my friends more than myself. They'd been put in harm's way for nothing more than being associated with me.

"Well, I suppose we should at least be grateful you weren't marooned with them. You're safe and that's the most important thing." Ray paused, giving my parents a moment to express their relief that I was unharmed and would soon be on my way back to the castle before he got back down to the business at hand—our rescue. "Do you know where you are?"

"I'm not sure, Ray. We don't have a map or anything useful to determine our coordinates. Is there anything you can do to triangulate the call?" My security team had all the latest technology at their disposal. If there was a way to trace our call, Ray had the equipment to do it.

"Here, maybe there's something on this that will help." Erin grabbed the pamphlet from the honeymoon reality TV show and handed it to me.

I read off all the pertinent information listed on the brochure and ended the call with Ray. The cavalry was on its way. We were as good as rescued. All that was left to do was collect the few belongings we had and make our way back down to the beach. We needed to get a head start on the helicopter. It would take hours for the rescue team to arrive, but moving Silas down to the shore meant for a slow hike down the hillside.

Once we reached the beach, we decided to double down and build a signal fire, making it easier for the rescue team to find the remote island. Viktor and I gathered as much driftwood and kindling as we could, piled it high and used the matches from the cabin. The fire began to spark, and after several minutes of letting it burn, we tossed green palm leaves on top to create a massive plume of smoke.

And then we waited.

The whirring thump of the helicopter blades chopping through the air and whipping up whitecaps on the water was a welcome sound and sight. As much as I wanted to stay, the danger of infection in Silas's wounds grew with every day that passed on the island.

Ray dropped out of the helicopter and waited for one of the crew members to lower a basket while Viktor and I carried Silas to be loaded in first. Once we had him situated, the medic began treating his injuries, starting a round of preventive antibiotics and making him more comfortable with pain medication. Erin, Viktor and I boarded the chopper and left the island, along with our time together, behind.

The welcome party awaiting us near the landing pad on the castle grounds consisted of my mother and father, my brother Nickolai and Posey. Some were happier than others to see us return from our disaster at sea. Each had his or her own reasons.

My parents were relieved and delighted that I was safe and sound. My companions, the source of numerous scandalous headlines across Europe, however, were another story altogether. They were quick to dismiss Erin, Viktor and Silas to a guest wing as far from the public eye as possible, with strict instructions to stay there—out of sight and out of mind of my parents—until travel arrangements could be made. Guards were stationed at the entrance of the wing to ensure only those with explicit permission from the king and queen were granted access to our guests.

I couldn't help but wonder if my name was included on that exclusive list.

Posey's relief was genuine, but I suspected she would have been equally relieved if I had not returned from the deserted island. We were friends, and I did not doubt that she cared for my wellbeing and would never wish me harm, but she wasn't eager to be wed any more than I was. Neither was Posey's girlfriend eager for us to be wed. They had been in a long-term relationship, and while she had agreed to be the princess's royal mistress, she was less than thrilled with the situation. The same could be said for Posey and her obligations to her country and mine. Still, she would do her duty.

As would I.

Nickolai never bothered to hide his disappointment. His sour face matched his mood and the smell of alcohol on his breath. According to Ray, he'd been on a bender since our distress call was received. As far as he was concerned, I was the one thing that stood in his way to claiming the throne and ruling over Liechtenstein. He was a king in his own mind, but never would be in the hearts of our people. My brother was cruel, juvenile and lacked the overall character of a royal heir. Never mind the ruler of our nation. But that never stopped his grandiose plans for ruining my life and my future place on the throne.

The drones and smear campaign in the tabloids had been his last attempt at destroying my character and supplanting himself on the throne. Additionally, I had my suspicions that he was somehow involved in the kidnapping and ransom attempt that landed us on that island in the first place. I couldn't blame Nickolai for the storm that destroyed the small yacht, but the idea that he had somehow been involved with the captain and crew plagued me from the moment I washed up on that shore.

Erin's friend, Bree, had been the one light in an ever-darkening tunnel. She left everything behind in the States and flew across Europe when news of the shipwreck reached her. She'd been waiting at a hotel in the village of Schaanwald, contacting our security through the guards stationed at the main gate for daily updates, until Posey arranged for her to be taken to the palace grounds.

Watching their reunion was the most joy I'd felt upon our return. Regardless of what became of her relationship with Viktor and Silas, I felt certain Erin would have the support she needed in her friend.

After a visit with the palace doctor to satisfy my parents' fears that I hadn't picked up a disease or parasite in the tropical climate, I mentally prepared myself to say my goodbyes and made my way across the palace to the guest wing.

"Are we prisoners here or what, man?" Viktor answered my knock at the door and ushered me inside their so-called prison cell.

"Don't get me wrong, the room service is a hell of a lot better than a county lock-up." Silas laughed and raised his hands in the air at Erin's chagrined look. "Not that I know from experience or anything. I'm just guessing."

"Of course, not." I gave them my best assurances that their travel arrangements were made, and they would be back in the States by the following evening. "This is just a precaution. I would never allow any harm to come to you. I hope you'll forgive my parents' overprotectiveness, but after everything that transpired since I left for our holiday—"

"Oh, don't listen to them, Henryk. Of course, we understand. Between the tabloids and the kidnappers, I'm surprised the king and queen let you out of their sight long enough to come see us." Erin rushed over and pulled me into a hug. "I was afraid I wouldn't get to see you before we left."

"I couldn't let you go without saying goodbye, Erin." I spared a glance over the top of her golden locks at Viktor and Silas. "And the two of you as well. I want to thank you for convincing me to go to Ibiza with you."

"But maybe not on the boat," Silas teased his best friend about the last leg of our journey and the greatest, most dangerous leg of our adventure.

"No, definitely not the boat," I confirmed with a laugh, and buried my face in the crook of Erin's neck, breathing her in one last time.

"I can't believe this is really the end." Erin pulled back from our embrace and wiped a tear from her eye with the back of her hand. "I mean, deep down I knew that it couldn't last forever, but I hoped it would, you know?"

She turned and walked across the suite to Bree, who waited with open arms to console her friend. Something she seemed to have experience with and knew just the right words to say to soothe Erin's broken heart and frazzled nerves. I envied Bree's ability to do so and longed to be the one holding Erin, making promises that everything would be okay.

But that would have been a lie because nothing would ever be okay again. Not once she stepped on the private jet and flew across the Atlantic and out of my life forever.

A knock sounded at the door.

"I'm starting to feel like the damned butler around here." Viktor marched toward the door, gesturing to me on his way. "You want to get it? It's probably for you anyway."

"Viktor. So lovely to see you again." Posey strolled into the room dressed to the nines in designer clothes and priceless jewels. She was stunning, but there wasn't enough silk or diamonds in the world for her to hold a candle when compared to Erin. My fiancée nodded to the other guests in the room. "Silas, Erin, Bree, Viktor. I hope the suites are to your liking."

"Everything is wonderful, thanks." Bree smiled and jumbled through a curtsey as she clutched Erin's hand. "But I'll be glad to get back home to my lumpy mattress and overpriced apartment."

"And bacon cheeseburgers with a double side of fries," Silas chimed in. "The caviar and champagne are great, but I could go for a hot grill and an ice-cold beer."

At least they had something to look forward to.

They all had lives to go back to, and no matter how much I wanted them here with me, it would have been selfish to ask them to stay. Especially when I couldn't accept them in my life publicly, and I refused to place them in a situation where they had anything to feel ashamed about.

Because there was nothing shameful in loving someone. Or three someones.

"Well, as lovely as that sounds, I'll have to take your word for it." Posey ran her fingers along the string of diamonds that dangled from her neck and smiled. "I'm definitely a champagne and caviar girl myself. But I'm afraid your dreams of hamburgers will have to wait. The queen has asked for Henryk's presence. She's making an announcement, and I thought it might be fun if you were all present."

"Fun?" I arched a brow at my fiancée. I knew that look in her eyes. She'd gotten into her share of mischief over the years that we'd known each other. "What are you up to?"

"You'll just have to wait and see. I don't want to spoil the surprise." Posey strolled to the door and held it open, something she would never have done under normal circumstances. "She's in her office. Lead the way, Your Highness."

Whatever Posey had planned, I was certain my mother wouldn't approve. For once, I was happy to be called to my mother's office.

Entourage in tow, I led the way across the palace, down numerous corridors to the official offices of Her Royal Highness, the Queen of Liechtenstein.

"Mother, you requested my presence," I announced myself and escorted everyone into the business suite.

"I requested your presence, yes." She watched with wary eyes as my group of friends filed into her office. "The emphasis being on *your presence.*"

"Whatever you have to say to me, you can say in front of them." I straightened my spine, standing at my full height, and braced for the impact of her announcement.

"If you insist." She let out a heavy sigh and reclaimed her seat behind her desk. "I called you here to discuss the upcoming nuptials. My secretary is drafting a formal announcement as we speak, and the planning committee has begun preparations for the date we selected prior to your little holiday."

I should have known that was what she wanted to discuss with me. Once she realized that I was alive and physically able to walk down the aisle, nothing would stop her from marrying me off and securing the line of succession.

"That's wonderful news, Your Highness," Posey stepped in, answering for me as I stood mute across from my mother's desk. "Henryk and I are ecstatic. And if you'll permit me, I have an announcement of my own."

The queen waved a dismissive hand, encouraging my fiancée to get on with whatever it was she wanted to say. If it wasn't related to the wedding, my mother didn't seem at all concerned about it.

But something about Posey's demeanor and the wicked glint in her eyes said that she should be concerned. Very concerned.

"As a show of my gratitude for their aid in ensuring my dear fiancé was unharmed while stranded on that horrible island, I've invited the Americans to the wedding." Posey clasped her hands together with overstated enthusiasm. "But that's not even the best part. They've also agreed to help with the preparations. I am so looking forward to having a western flare at the reception."

My mother paled at the news. So much so, that I considered calling the royal doctor to have her examined for fear that she may have gone into shock. But ever the stoic queen, she was quick to regain her composure and put on her best public smile.

"How wonderful." The queen glared at Posey over the rim of her horn-rimmed glasses and shuffled the papers on her massive oak desk. "I look forward to reviewing their recommendations with the planning committee. Henryk, will you be joining your father and me for dinner this evening?"

It was a request, but one I knew not to deny. Posey's ploy would not go unchallenged. My mother was shrewd enough to wait until she had me alone and reinforcements on her side. Namely, my father.

Still, Posey had given me an early wedding gift. More time with Erin, Viktor and Silas. Time that I fully intended to make the most of. My fiancée was up to something. Of that I was sure, but I was more than willing to play the game because I had too much to lose.

And if I won, I could have my wedding cake and eat it too.